BIONICLE®

RAID ON VULCANUS

BIONICLE®

RAID ON VULCANUS

BY GREG FARSHTEY

SCHOLASTIC INC.

NEW YORK   TORONTO   LONDON   AUCKLAND   SYDNEY
MEXICO CITY   NEW DELHI   HONG KONG   BUENOS AIRES

ISBN-13: 978-0-545-10073-1   ISBN-10: 0-545-10073-9

12 11 10 9 8 7 6 5 4 3 2   9 10 11 12 13 14/0

Book design by Henry Ng
Printed in the U.S.A.
First printing, July 2009

BIONICLE®

RAID ON VULCANUS

CHARACTER
GUIDE

ACKAR
Village: Vulcanus
Occupation: Glatorian
Weapons: Flame sword; spiked
Thornax launcher

Ackar is a legend among Glatorian
and probably the most talented
fighter since the days of Certavus.
Lately his skills have slipped. Although
he is still considered the top fighter
in Vulcanus, he now spends time
training new Glatorian.

FERO
Village: Roxtus
Occupation: Bone Hunter
Weapons: Sword; spiked Thornax
launcher

Fero is a respected and feared
member of the Bone Hunters,
nomadic raiders who stalk the Bara
Magna desert. Alone or with his tribe,
he attacks trade caravans, traveling
Glatorian, and villages.

GELU

Village: Iconox
Occupation: Armed guard for hire; former Glatorian
Weapons: Ice slicer; spiked Thornax launcher

Gelu is resourceful, quick, and always looking
for a way to make a quick profit. As a Glatorian,
Gelu was fairly successful. When the Skrall sacked
the city of Atero, Gelu "retired" and went into
business as an armed escort for Agori who
needed to cross the desert.

GRESH

Village: Tesara
Occupation: Glatorian
Weapons: Shield; spiked Thornax launcher

Gresh is a young Glatorian who is noble, smart,
and has little patience for cheaters or thieves.
He has won a number of important matches
for Tesara. Gresh believes Glatorian have a
responsibility to do more than just fight for pay.

KIINA

Village: Tajun
Occupation: Glatorian
Weapons: Dual-headed vapor trident; spiked
Thornax launcher

Kiina is the most successful female Glatorian in
the history of Bara Magna. She is wisecracking
and temperamental, but she's a loyal friend to those
she respects. Kiina is closest to Ackar and Gresh.

MALUM

Village: None
Occupation: Former Glatorian
Weapons: Flame claws; spiked Thornax launcher

Malum was once a valued Glatorian for the village of Vulcanus. During a match, he attempted to kill his opponent after he had already surrendered. Malum was exiled from his village as punishment.

METUS

Village: Iconox
Occupation: Glatorian promoter and trainer
Weapons: Ice axe; shield

Metus is good at two things. The first is recognizing talented Glatorian. The second is making deals. He travels the desert looking for talent and setting up matches between the Glatorian of various villages.

RAANU

Village: Vulcanus
Occupation: Village elder
Weapons: Fire blade; shield

Raanu is the leader of Vulcanus.
He does his best to keep his
people safe. That is getting
harder to do with Bone
Hunters prowling in the desert,
hungry Vorox in the wastelands,
and brutal Skrall moving down
from the north.

STRAKK

Village: Iconox
Occupation: Glatorian
Weapons: Ice axe; spiked
Thornax launcher

Strakk is a veteran of the Spherus
Magna conflict. During those hard
years, he learned to look out
only for himself. As a Glatorian,
he hasn't changed. He fights for
money and will use his weapon for
anyone willing to pay for it.

TARIX
Village: Tajun
Occupation: Glatorian
Weapons: Twin water blades; spiked Thornax launcher

Along with the legendary Certavus, Tarix was one of the founders of the Glatorian system on Bara Magna. Of living Glatorian, only Ackar has been a Glatorian champion more often than Tarix.

VASTUS
Village: Tesara
Occupation: Glatorian
Weapons: Snake venom talon; spiked Thornax launcher

Vastus was a field commander in the war on Spherus Magna. When that conflict led to a horrible disaster, Vastus vowed to make sure the people of Tesara would always be protected.

ONE

Fero reined Skirmix to a halt and scanned the horizon. Little was moving on the sands of Bara Magna this day. Here and there, a Zesk crawled out of the sand in search of a meal. Scavenger birds wheeled in the sky, waiting for something to drop from the heat. The emptiness of the desert was no surprise. It was high sun, and only lunatics and fools would be out in this heat.

But the armored warrior was neither crazy nor stupid. Fero had a job to do. Any rider or caravan forced to travel at this time of day would be moving slowly — too slowly to evade a determined hunter.

He checked his weaponry. His blade was scored by sand and carried the scars of hundreds of battles, but it was still razor sharp. He had found it in the ruins of a Glatorian training arena

1

a long time back. With luck, today it would help him in another successful hunt.

His rock steed growled. It didn't like to stand still. Its body was designed to be self-cooling, but only if it kept on the move. Fero was about to spur on his mount when Skirmix began shaking its head and snapping its jaws together. The animal sensed prey.

Like all Bone Hunters, Fero had a second set of eyelids, which shielded his eyes from the sun. He closed them now, reducing the sun's glare. Yes, there was something out there, far to the west. It was a lone transport driven by Agori villagers from Iconox. Riding alongside was a single Glatorian whom Fero recognized instantly.

Gelu, the Hunter said to himself. *Then this hunt is both business and pleasure.*

The Glatorian named Gelu was feeling pleased with himself this day. Even the extreme heat and the stench of the sand stalker he rode could not ruin his mood. He was, after all, on his way to becoming very rich.

For most of Bara Magna, the past few days had been nightmarish. For many years, the southern villages had enjoyed an uneasy peace with Roxtus, the Skrall city to the north. Skrall warriors dominated the Glatorian battles in the arenas, but in general, they followed the rules and respected the rights of other villages. Now all that had changed.

The changes happened little by little. First, the Skrall started challenging places like Tajun and Vulcanus to matches to win anything, from caches of arms and equipment to access to oases and trade routes. Since the peoples of Bara Magna relied on Glatorian fights to settle their disputes, rejecting a Skrall challenge was impossible. The results of the battles were always the same: the Skrall would win and take what they wanted.

Then the Skrall got more aggressive. They started claiming land and resources without bothering to fight in the arena for them. When they did fight, they sometimes killed their opponents, later claiming the Glatorian deaths were just "unfortunate accidents." Meanwhile, Glatorian fighters traveling between villages started disappearing. True, the wastelands were always dangerous, but too many were vanishing for it to be a coincidence.

Things came to a climax during the annual Glatorian tournament in the village of Atero. Everyone wondered what was going on when no Skrall fighters arrived to participate. They found out when an army of Skrall descended on the village, destroying the great arena and killing many Glatorian. Their days of pretending to be part of Bara Magna society were over. The Skrall had declared war.

Disaster for some, though, meant opportunity for others. Gelu now hired himself out as a bodyguard for Agori trade caravans and other travelers. He pledged to defend them against Skrall raiding parties, hungry Vorox, Bone Hunters, and any other threats. He also made sure he got paid up front.

The sand stalker snorted and reared. Gelu could see why. There were signs of a battle having been fought here. Broken weapons and shattered armor were scattered in the sand. The stalker could smell death, and it didn't like the scent.

The villagers making up the transport were paler than their white armor. They were carrying badly needed goods to Tajun. Caravans to that village had become a prime target for Bone Hunters. The last three that went without Glatorian protection had never arrived.

"Relax," said Gelu. "I've traveled this route a dozen times in the last two weeks. Outside of a few Zesk scavengers, I haven't run into anything worth fighting."

The driver nodded. "Tell that to the traders who vanished out here."

"Sand seas," offered Gelu. "Storms. Maybe rockslides, if they went through the mountains. Lots of dangers out here — not just Skrall and Bone Hunters."

This, of course, was only half true. There were plenty of threats in the wastelands, from weather to wildlife. But Tajun-bound traders were being picked off by Bone Hunters, and everyone knew it. Still, why bring it up? It might frighten the customers. And frightened customers turn back and want their payment returned.

The Spikit pulling the wagon gave a menacing hiss. It was a two-headed reptilian creature, not too fast, but tough and aggressive. As long as it was well-fed, it would defend a wagon to the death. Let it get hungry, though, and it would eat your trade goods, your wagon, and you, not necessarily in that order. Growling from a Spikit meant one of two things: it sensed danger, or it had missed a meal.

Gelu scanned the sands. His eye caught a glint of sunlight on dull metal. He knew he was looking at a Bone Hunter. The good news was that there was only one. The bad news was that one was more than enough to make serious trouble.

The Glatorian spoke in a calm, steady voice, without turning to look at the Agori. "When I give the word, take off as fast as two-head can pull you. There's a sandstorm building to the west. If need be, you can hide inside it. I'll be along soon."

"What is it?" asked one of the villagers. "Are we in danger?"

"Agori, you've been in danger since before Bara Magna had moons. Now do as I say."

The Bone Hunter was on the move now, riding down from the high dunes. Gelu gave a yell, and the Agori started their transport moving. Gelu waited a few seconds to make sure they were well on their way before riding up to meet the Hunter.

By the time he reached Fero, Gelu wore a bitter smile of recognition. The two of them had clashed a number of times over the last few weeks. Sometimes Fero succeeded in smashing the caravan and stealing or destroying the goods. Other times, Gelu got his clients away clean. He had learned the hard way about having the Agori stand and fight. Better to let them risk the sands than face Fero.

"They'll be long gone by the time you finish with me," said Gelu.

"How do you know there aren't more Bone Hunters waiting to ambush them?" Fero replied.

Gelu laughed. "They're carrying a small fortune in food, spare parts, and whatever else they can trade in Tajun — and you don't like to share."

Fero suddenly swung his blade. Gelu ducked just before it took his head off. Skirmix snapped its jaws, trying to get at Gelu's sand stalker, but the stalker backed away and kicked. Its hoof struck Skirmix in the left knee, and the creature lurched.

Fero had to drop his guard in order to grab onto the reins. Gelu hit him in the side with the flat of his ice blade, sending him tumbling off Skirmix. But Fero rolled on impact and came up on his feet. He aimed his Thornax launcher right at Gelu.

"Get down," Fero snarled.

Gelu slipped down to the sand and faced Fero.

"Now toss your launcher far away," said

the Bone Hunter, his own launcher never wavering.

Not seeing any other choice, Gelu hurled his launcher to the side. He still had his ice blade. To his surprise, Fero did the same. The two faced each other armed only with swords.

Fero struck first and fast, driving Gelu back with a series of hard strikes. After only a few minutes of fighting, Gelu's arms were starting to feel like they were made of rock. The heat was getting to him. He had to finish this blade fight fast, or he was the one who would be finished.

Sensing his opponent's weakness, Fero bore down. He wasn't going to give Gelu time to recover. He forced the Glatorian back, and back again.

Then Gelu unexpectedly ducked and kicked up his legs. He caught Fero in the midsection and propelled him into the air. Fero landed face-first in a dune while Gelu scrambled to his feet. He glanced to the side to ensure his sand stalker was keeping Skirmix out of the battle.

The Bone Hunter was starting to get up. Gelu took a few quick steps and kicked Fero's sword away from him. That was when he spotted something else on the sand. It was a piece of parchment with what looked like a map drawn on it. Keeping his blade close enough to strike Fero if he made a move, he picked it up.

A swift scan showed it was a detailed map of the village of Vulcanus. There were a series of dates down the side with a number beside each.

"What is this?" asked Gelu.

"Go to the sand bog," Fero spat. "I'm not telling you anything."

Gelu snatched up his Thornax launcher and aimed it toward Skirmix. "Want to walk home?"

Fero looked at his mount, then back at Gelu. His expression was as cold as Iconox ice. "If I have to."

Gelu frowned. It was said that a Bone Hunter's jaws could clamp shut tighter than a rock dragon's on a meal. If Fero didn't want to talk, he wasn't going to. Gelu wondered if he should kill the Bone Hunter, but decided against it. It would only paint a target on his back for every other member of Fero's tribe.

Gelu got back on his sand stalker. He fired a Thornax above Skirmix's head and one right in front of his nose. The beast backed off a half-dozen paces. Then Gelu urged his mount forward. The sand stalker stepped on Fero's launcher, producing a very satisfying crunch.

"You might want to start learning to share," said Gelu, as he rode away.

By the time he caught up to the transport, it was in pretty bad shape. A small band of Zesk had appeared out of the sand and made off with more than half of its contents before the Agori villagers could scare them off. They grumbled about being left to defend themselves. Gelu reminded them that Bone Hunters don't scare as easily as Zesk. Fero wouldn't have left them anything, including their lives.

The remaining ride to Tajun was uneventful and gave Gelu time to study the map he had taken from Fero. It seemed strange. For one thing, Bone Hunters usually wrote in their own language, which was different from Agori. It would be almost impossible for an outsider to read. Once or twice he had seen a Hunter carrying something with Skrall markings on it, most likely found when riding around the northern wastes near Roxtus. Bone Hunters wouldn't be stupid enough to attack the fierce Skrall warriors, but weren't above looting dead ones.

The notes scrawled on this map, however, were in perfect Agori. It was more than just a standard map of how to get to and from Vulcanus. Each outer wall was marked, along with every other defense the village had in place. Gelu had been to the village a week before, and there were things on this chart that hadn't been there then. This has to be a brand-new document. But how did it get in the hands of a Bone Hunter?

Gelu was still pondering these questions as he walked the streets of Tajun. The village consisted of a single massive structure beneath which were a series of small, crudely made shelters.

Tajun was located on top of an oasis, so water was never an issue for the residents. For everything else, they relied on trade. With the Bone Hunters' interference in recent months, the villagers were hurting. Even the small amount of goods in the Iconox transport was welcome.

Gelu spotted Metus, an Agori from his village. Metus was a Glatorian trainer and promoter. He traveled Bara Magna looking for good fighters and set up matches between villages. For him, Tajun was now the place to be.

"Never saw anything like it," he said to Gelu. "These people need everything — food, tools, spare parts, you name it — and they're willing to take challenges to get them. Tarix and Kiina have had six matches in the last week. They're both starting to wear out."

Gelu could understand that. The two Glatorian were both veteran fighters, but at that pace, and with so much riding on each match, anyone would get run down.

13

"Hey," said Metus, eyeing Gelu as if for the first time. "You're pretty good in the arena. Tajun will give you double what Iconox does if you win a few for them."

Gelu shook his head. "Sorry, Metus, I'm out of that game . . . for now. I like doing escort work. Keeps me on the move."

"Got it," Metus replied, after a momentary look of disappointment. "Well, if you change your mind. . . . So far, all I've managed to recruit is a kid named Gresh from Tesara. Not bad — still needs training, but not bad. We're headed to Vulcanus for a match today."

Gelu remembered the map in his bag. Someone in Vulcanus would probably be very interested in seeing it. And Gelu had to admit that he was intrigued by the mystery himself.

"A lot of Bone Hunters between here and there," he said. "You could use an extra sword. Mind if I tag along?"

TWO

Beyond a brief greeting when he and Gelu were introduced, Gresh didn't say much during the first part of the journey. Normally, Gelu would have written this off as nerves. Young Glatorian did one of two things around veterans: they asked questions non-stop, or shut up completely, afraid to sound stupid if they opened their mouths.

But Gresh wasn't a typical newcomer to the game. He had won all but one of his matches for Tesara, and the one he lost was to a Skrall warrior. There was no shame in that. Back when Roxtus sent fighters to the arena, no one had ever beaten a Skrall.

Gelu liked the kid. Too many young fighters thought being a Glatorian was all about profit or personal glory. But the best of the breed knew it was a lot more than that.

15

"Who are you fighting?" he asked Gresh.

Before Gresh could answer, Metus did it for him. "He's fighting Ackar. You know they kicked Malum out, right? He killed an opponent who had already surrendered. So they're down to Ackar and a couple of kids who are still so new they don't know which end of the sword to hold."

Gelu had done more than hear about Malum. He had spotted the crimson-armored ex-Glatorian a few times out in the wastelands. He had no idea how Malum was surviving out there on his own. But the look Gelu had seen in his eyes said maybe it was better not to know.

"Up ahead," Gresh broke in. "Looks like trouble."

The kid had good eyes. Far off in the distance, an Agori transport had lost a wheel. The two drivers, both from Vulcanus, were struggling to get it back on while trying not to get too close to their hungry Spikit. As the Glatorian approached, one of the Agori looked up at

Gelu. Then he looked away, shaking his head in disgust.

"Another Glatorian from Iconox," the villager said. "He won't help. Keep working."

"You don't think too highly of the ice village, I'm guessing?" said Gelu.

"We broke down two hours ago," said the other Agori. "Not long after, a Glatorian from your village comes by. He offers to patch the transport and get us to Vulcanus. But says he's pretty sure the pass ahead is full of Vorox, so his price is half the goods we're carrying. We said no."

Vorox were residents of a sand village who had backslid after the disasters of 100,000 years back. Now they were little more than beasts, hiding in the desert and pouncing on anyone who passed through their hunting grounds. If a traveler was lucky, he only lost his transport and his goods. If he wasn't, well, then he wouldn't have to worry about the heat anymore.

"Maybe 'yes' would have been a better answer," Gelu said.

"Vorox? Did they say Vorox?" said Metus, trying to look in every direction at once. "Let's go. These guys will be fine. We'll take the long way."

To Gelu's surprise, Gresh dismounted from his sand stalker. "No. We'll help," the kid said.

The Agori put his hands on his hips, a look of defiance in his eyes. "We can't afford you. Move on and let us get back to work."

"No one wants your goods," Gresh answered. "Stay here and you'll be dead before another sunrise."

"Wait a minute!" Metus said. "What am I hearing? Tell me you just want to fix the wheel, and then we move on."

Gresh turned and looked at the promoter. When he spoke, his voice was quiet and even. "No. We're going to fix the transport and then get them to Vulcanus. It's the right thing to do."

Gelu smiled. He respected Gresh's guts, if not his sense of fair odds. He was one Glatorian with two Agori about to go up against potentially dozens of Vorox. It was suicide. Then again, Gelu remembered taking the same kind of foolish chances when he started out.

"You're going to need an extra set of eyes," he said, getting down off his sand stalker. "If you don't watch both flanks, the Vorox will be on you before you can raise your shield."

"I don't believe this!" sputtered Metus. "You're crazy, the both of you! Gresh, your village is counting on you — do you have any idea how upset Tesara will be with me if you get killed because you wanted to do someone a favor?"

Gelu laughed. "Don't worry about it, Metus. If this goes bad, odds are none of us will be alive to take the heat for it. So get down and help with this wheel, okay?"

Repairs to the wagon went quickly, but it was still a little too close to sunset for anyone's liking. Metus suggested they make camp and set out in the morning, but Gresh disagreed.

"We have a better chance of making it through if we are mounted and moving," he said. "There's no shelter here, nothing but sand. They could come up from underneath us whenever they wanted."

Gresh and Gelu got back on their mounts. Both checked their Thornax launchers to make sure they were ready to go. Gelu scanned the pass up ahead, but couldn't see any Vorox. That meant nothing, of course — by the time you saw them, it was usually too late.

"Let's go," said Gelu. He turned to the two Agori drivers. "If it comes to it, you jump on our sand stalkers and leave the transport. No matter what you're carrying, it's not worth your lives."

The group moved out, traveling from sunlight into shadow. Gresh kept his eyes straight ahead, watching for movement in the sand that would signal Vorox about to emerge from below. Gelu swept his gaze over the rocks on either side.

Something gleamed in the fading sunlight on a high slope. "Up ahead, on the right," Gelu said quietly.

"I see it," Gresh replied.

A Vorox suddenly appeared, blade in hand,

right where Gelu had indicated. The Glatorian aimed and fired his launcher in one swift motion, winging the bestial warrior.

A sword flew down from the left side of the pass, burying itself in the sand in front of Gresh's mount. His sand stalker reared and almost threw him, but the Glatorian got it back under control. Metus looked at the weapon as they passed, his eyes wide.

"This is crazy," he muttered. "We're not going to make it through here."

"Sure, we are," said Gelu, smiling. "Just stay calm, Metus. Try not to look too appetizing, and you'll be fine."

"Left side!" snapped Gresh.

Gelu spun and quickly fired three spiked spheres from his launcher. He hit two of the Vorox that Gresh had spotted. The third ducked back behind the rocks. A soft sound made Gelu turn around just in time to spot another Vorox coming out of the sand. He swung his ice blade and disarmed it, then knocked it unconscious with a second blow.

Vorox began filing out of the rocks on both sides like insects from a disturbed sand hill. Gresh and Gelu used their launchers to try to keep them pinned down, but they were already leaping from ledges and charging across the sand. As soon as the Vorox were close enough to make this a hand-to-hand fight, it would be over.

Seeking some way the party could escape, Gelu's eyes fell on the transport. Most of the items in it were old and battered, but there were two pieces of armor that looked close to new. He bent over as he rode past, snatching them up. Then he tossed one to Gresh. "The leader! Throw it!" he shouted.

Gresh got the idea. He tossed the piece of armor to the lead Vorox on the left, while Gelu did the same on the right. The Vorox grabbed the items out of the air. Instantly, the rest of the pack noticed that two of their number had treasures. They started grabbing for the pieces of armor. When the new owners resisted, things turned vicious. A mad scramble started, as each

Vorox who got his hands on the shiny items became a target for all the rest.

"Come on!" yelled Gelu. "This won't keep them busy for long!"

The Agori got the Spikit moving, while Gresh, Gelu, and Metus rode behind. No one slowed down until the pass was well behind them and smoke from the fires of Vulcanus was visible in the twilight sky.

Gelu looked back. No one was pursuing them. "Not bad," he said, turning back to Gresh. "You're pretty good in a fight, kid. If I were Ackar, I'd be worried."

The two Agori drivers couldn't meet the eyes of their Glatorian companions. Finally, one spoke up. "We . . . um . . . want to apologize. We thought you Glatorians fought only for money. I guess we were wrong."

"No, you weren't," said Metus. He glared at Gresh as he added, "That's the way it's *supposed* to be."

Gresh ignored him. Nodding to the Agori,

he turned his mount and rode toward Vulcanus. After a moment, Gelu joined him.

"So," said Gelu. "You do that sort of thing often?"

"When it's needed," Gresh answered. "I'm bigger, stronger, and faster than the Agori. I've got a shield and a launcher, and I know how to use them. I'm a Glatorian. Doesn't that mean I have to protect people who aren't as strong as I am?"

Gelu was silent for a moment. Then he said, "Tell me something, Gresh — are you sure you're from this planet?"

The rest of the ride to Vulcanus was uneventful. The two Glatorian shared a meal of burnt sand bat and talked at the village inn. Slowly at first, Gresh began to open up. He talked with Gelu about the challenges he had faced in the arena and his worries that someday he might let his village down. For a Glatorian, the outcome of a single battle could mean the difference between a village thriving or one just surviving.

"Listen, friend, anyone who ever picked up a sword to fight for one of these sand pits has felt the same way," said Gelu. "Sometimes, it's easy to forget why Glatorian need to do what we do — even the Agori sometimes forget what started it all. Heck, I wish I could."

"You were there when . . . ?" Gresh began.

Gelu nodded. "Oh, yeah, I was there, along with many others. Six armies, all fighting over a glittering silver liquid that changed or destroyed whatever it touched — some saw it as a power source, others as a weapon. Battles raged all across the planet, going back and forth, until somebody, somewhere, figured out a way to tap that power. And . . . well, you know the rest. . . . The planet wound up in pieces."

The Iconox Glatorian looked around the inn. Agori were eating, talking, most of them in battered armor that should have been replaced ages ago. It was easy to see the places where the metal was patched, often with scraps that didn't quite match the original color. No one looked particularly happy or sad. Mostly, they just looked tired.

"That was, what, more than one hundred thousand years ago now?" Gelu continued. "Agori scattered all over, finding shelter where they could. Villagers couldn't afford another war, even if anyone still had an appetite for one. So somebody got the bright idea to hire veteran warriors to fight on the villages' behalf. If Vulcanus and Tesara had a disagreement, well, each one hired a Glatorian and they'd fight it out. The winner got whatever he needed — food, shelter, weapons, armor. Keep winning and you could get rich — well, as rich as you can ever be out this way. But the trick was to keep winning."

"Is that why you quit?" Gresh asked. Seeing the look on Gelu's face, he said, "It's not a secret. Kiina told me last time I was in Tajun. She said she hadn't seen you in an arena in weeks."

Gelu smiled. "Yeah, Kiina would notice that. It's simple — nobody is going to be on top forever. Look at Ackar. They love him here now — they *need* him now — but watch him lose a few matches and see how fast he gets pushed aside. I decided I didn't want to wait for that to happen to me — not when there's so much money to be made getting people and things from place to place."

Even as he said that, Gelu spotted Raanu coming into the inn. Raanu was the elder of the village of Vulcanus. He was tough and honest, even if sometimes stubborn beyond belief. He was also the keeper of anything of value in the place, which made him just the person Gelu needed to see.

"Excuse me," he said to Gresh as he rose. "I have to see an Agori about a map."

⟯ T H R E E ⟮

"This is bad. This is very, very bad," said Raanu. He looked up at Gelu and waved the map. "Do you know what this is?"

"Bad?" offered Gelu.

"Worse than bad," muttered the village elder. "There are walls on this map that didn't even exist two weeks ago. With something like this, the Bone Hunters could go around or through any of our defenses. We wouldn't stand a chance."

"Good thing I found it for you then," Gelu said. He waited then, eyes on Raanu. The elder would have to offer him some kind of reward for his service . . . wouldn't he?

But Raanu was paying no attention to the expectant Glatorian. He was looking at his people gathered in the inn and wondering how many would survive a Skrall attack. Not many, he guessed.

"A few Thornax launchers, some swords and spears, picks, shovels, hammers," he said quietly. "That's not going to stop those barbarians. They will ride in, take whatever we have, and leave us with nothing — that's if they don't burn the whole village down."

Gelu had to agree. He had seen firsthand what Bone Hunters could do. No bunch of Agori, no matter how determined, would be able to stand up to a raiding party . . . not in direct combat, anyway.

"We may have to flee," Raanu said, voice heavy with despair. "Go out into the wastelands and start again, maybe further south. Maybe if we let them have what they want, they'll leave us alone."

"Not likely." The words came from Gresh, who had wandered over to find out what had upset Raanu. "If the Bone Hunters know you're afraid of them, they'll keep after you until you drop dead in the sand."

"But we *are* afraid of them," said Raanu. "And with good reason! It would take an army to stop them, and in case you didn't notice, we have no army."

Gelu started to reply, then stopped. He had to think hard about his next words. They might land him in the middle of a bad situation. Then again, if he didn't say them, Gresh would. At least if he did it first, he might be able to negotiate a fee.

"You don't need an army," Gelu said. "You need Glatorian — good ones, fast, experienced. A small team might not be able to defeat a legion of Bone Hunters, but they can make the fight so costly for them that they'll turn back."

Raanu beckoned for Gelu to go on, but it was Gresh who spoke. "I get it. Stall them. Trick them. Trap them."

Gelu nodded. "Right. Ever try to get a dune spider out from under a rock? It sprouts thorns all over its body and legs. Eventually, you give up and go find easier prey. You need to make Vulcanus too prickly to hold."

Raanu smiled. "Yes, yes . . . I like this idea. We'll make them wish they never came here. Let them raid some other village instead — Vulcanus will not surrender! And you, Gelu? You will lead these Glatorian?"

Gelu was ready for this question. He would act humbled by the suggestion, make a show of thinking about it, then agree — after, of course, Raanu had made a very generous offer. "Me?" he began, looking down at the floor. "Well, I don't know, Raanu. I'm not really in that business anymore, and —"

"He won't do it. I will. It's my job."

All three turned. Ackar was standing in the doorway. If any Glatorian could be considered a living legend, it was he. Even those who had never fought him knew his reputation. He was older now, maybe not as fearsome as in centuries past, but when he spoke, other Glatorian always listened.

"Ackar," said Raanu, seeming a little

embarrassed. "I was just about to go get you." He handed Ackar the map and explained the situation. The veteran Glatorian said nothing, just nodded slightly as he scanned the parchment.

"Not sure I agree with Gelu," Ackar finally said. "I've seen three Hunters decimate an entire caravan . . . six destroy an outpost. What happens if they come at you with twenty, thirty, or forty of their number? What then?"

Raanu looked stricken. "So you're saying we should give up? Flee?" Gelu had to suppress a smile on hearing the outrage in Raanu's voice. Five minutes ago, it was the Agori who had suggested that same strategy. Now he acted shocked to hear someone else say the same thing.

"I said I didn't agree with his idea," Ackar snapped. "I didn't say we wouldn't do it. We need an army, but we haven't got one. So we'll have to make do with what we have."

"I'm in," said Gresh. "This isn't my village, but I won't stand around and let Bone Hunters take it."

Ackar looked at Gelu. "How about you?"

Three Glatorian against any number of Bone Hunters? Crazy. This isn't what he had in mind. He'd had it all figured. Raanu would agree to the idea and hire Gelu to go out and recruit Glatorian, for a nice price. He would earn a good sum and not take too much of a risk. But with Ackar insisting on defending the village with the Glatorian they had, things were different. Still, if he turned down the request to defend the village, he could forget ever showing his mask here again.

"Okay," Gelu said. "Count me in, too." He didn't add that he felt like his heart had become a block of ice or that he was already sweating under his armor. It wasn't good to let other Glatorian know you were afraid.

"We'll send the two Glatorian trainees we have here to Tajun tonight with a message for Kiina and Tarix — neither would miss a fight if they can help it," Ackar said. "Gresh, head back to Tesara, find Vastus and whoever else you can. Gelu, you're with me."

"Do you think it's smart to leave the village undefended?" asked Gresh.

"One or two Glatorian won't stop the Bone Hunters," said Ackar. "We need more — a lot more. And we need them now."

Gresh glanced out the doorway to the charred and blackened main street of the village. "By now, Fero has let his people know he lost the map."

"Right," said Ackar, "which means they know we'll be preparing for them. They are going to move fast. So we have to move faster. I don't like leaving the village undefended, but we need to find allies. We'll have to gamble that we make it back before the Bone Hunters arrive."

There was no time for farewells. Gresh mounted his sand stalker and rode north. The two rookie Glatorian headed west, with strict instructions from Ackar to stay together and to be careful. Darkness had fallen over Bara Magna. It was the most dangerous time to be out in the desert.

Despite asking repeatedly, Gelu had been unable to find out where he and Ackar were going. He waited impatiently while the veteran told Raanu where to post look-outs and what to do if any Bone Hunter scouts appeared on the horizon. If things got truly desperate, he and the villagers were to burn anything they couldn't carry, head south, double back under the cover of sandstorms, and hide in Iron Canyon. With luck, the Bone Hunters would keep heading south and find themselves in the Sea of Liquid Sand. "Remember, though, if they see one straggler heading for the canyon, they will know what you're doing," said Ackar. "Your lives won't be worth a grain of sand then."

Gelu had packed a few days' worth of supplies onto his mount. Ackar saw what he was doing and nodded approvingly. "Good idea. We can use the food for trade."

"I was planning to use it for eating," answered Gelu. "I find it works much better that way."

Ackar gave a bitter laugh. "You don't want to be fattening yourself up, Gelu . . . not where we're going."

"Good luck to you both," said Raanu. "The hopes of everyone in Vulcanus ride with you."

"Then I hope they don't need to eat," muttered Gelu. "'Cause that's out, I hear."

The two Glatorian struck out to the north. They rode in silence for a few hours until they reached the banks of the Skrall River. Once, enough water had flowed to provide for all the needs of nearby villages. Now it was barely a trickle, thanks to a dam built by the Skrall. Many Glatorian, including Ackar, had challenged the Skrall in the arena, over that dam. The Skrall won every time, and the dam stayed in place. Gelu expected they would cross and head northwest for Iconox, but instead, Ackar wheeled his mount to the northeast.

Now Gelu knew where they were going. And he didn't like it one bit.

"Ackar!" the ice Glatorian whispered.

"We're heading right for Bone Hunter territory. Their camp is only a couple days' ride from here."

"I know," Ackar answered. "We're going to stop and pick up a . . . friend. Then we're going to see if we can't stop their plans before they start."

"You're going to make an attack on the Bone Hunters?" Gelu asked in disbelief. He offered his launcher to Ackar. "Here. Why not just kill me now?"

"Relax," said Ackar. "They expect us to be hiding behind walls. The last thing on their minds is the possibility that we'll attack them."

"It was the last thing on my mind, too," replied Gelu. "What are we going to use for an army?"

Ackar looked at Gelu for a few moments in silence. Then he chuckled softly and said, "You don't want to know."

Gresh rode hard. Tesara was a long way away from Vulcanus. He hoped Vastus or some of the other Glatorian would be there when he arrived. If they were traveling to a match, he might never find them. The idea of returning to Ackar empty-handed was something he wouldn't accept.

He rode through lonely, barren country. Parts of Bara Magna had always been desert, but he had heard stories that some regions were once a little more green, like Tesara. The cataclysmic events that tore through the world 100 millennia ago had changed all that.

Not for the first time, he wondered about the Skrall. Everyone had known they existed, even before they moved south into the desert. Their homeland was said to be north of the Black Spike Mountains, near a volcanic region that dwarfed Vulcanus. They kept largely to themselves for thousands of years, shunning any contacts with Iconox or any of the northern villages.

Then all that changed. The Skrall stormed down from the north and made their home in the city of Roxtus, a ruin that they rebuilt. They restricted travel to their city, allowing only

Raid on Vulcanus

Glatorian coming to fight or select Agori trade caravans. Those who made the trip spoke of a huge arena almost as big as the one in Atero, of warriors everywhere they looked, and of Spikit and other vicious beasts unleashed on Glatorian for the amusement of the onlookers.

Many Glatorian who went there to fight never returned. The Skrall usually blamed this on "accidents," or insisted the fighter had been fine when he left the city and must have met with some mishap on his way back home. Those few warriors who went there and made it back insisted they would never return.

The presence of the Skrall made all the other villages uneasy. Many wondered why they had bothered to migrate to such a barren region in the first place. Had they used up their own resources? Been driven out by some natural disaster? Or was there a more sinister reason for their sudden arrival?

Maybe no one would ever know why the Skrall did what they did. What mattered was that, after a period of pretending to want to be a part of Bara Magna society, the Skrall had shown their true nature. They wanted to conquer this world, and they had the warriors and the will to do it. With the Bone Hunters making more and more raids every day on top of the Skrall threat, the villages were in terrible danger.

Gresh reined his mount to a stop. Why had the Bone Hunters worked so hard to cut off Tajun? And why would they be targeting Vulcanus? Bone Hunters went after travelers and trade caravans. They didn't attack entire villages. Sure, Atero had been raided and sacked, but that hadn't been the Bone Hunters.

It was the Skrall.

Could it be? He wanted to reject the whole idea. The Bone Hunters were nomadic and survived by stealing and worse. They had no use for alliances with any village or tribe. Nor would they need to team with the Skrall for their own security. No one knew the sands better than the Bone Hunters. If the Skrall took aim at them, they could vanish into the desert and never be found. It didn't make sense that they might be working with — or for — the Skrall.

But what if they were? That question pounded in his brain. If the Skrall combined their organization, their weaponry, their sheer power with the Bone Hunters' lightning tactics and knowledge of the region . . . it could be all over for every free village on Bara Magna.

All the more reason to get where I'm going and get help, he thought grimly, as he spurred on his sand stalker. *We need to stop them at Vulcanus now, and stop them for good.*

Fero heard riders, but he couldn't see them. Dawn was still a few hours away and even the keen vision of a Bone Hunter could not pierce the darkness completely. But he could hear the rapid beats of sand stalker hooves in the soft sand, and he could smell the exhaustion of the animals . . . and the fear of their riders.

He smiled. He knew from their frantic pace that their mission was urgent and from their scents that they had ridden a long distance. He knew the riders were wise, for this was a place in which to be very afraid.

Fero turned to look at his four companions. Each carried a darkfire torch, which provided warmth in the chill desert night, but gave off no light. They were all veteran Bone Hunters, out for a night raid. With the Vulcanus map no doubt in the hands of Raanu, the expectation was that the village would be sending out a call for help and not waiting for daylight to do it. Fero would be willing to bet a month's loot that the two riders down below had started from Vulcanus and were on their way to hire more Glatorian for the village's defense.

Too bad they were never going to reach their destination.

Fero gave a whispered command, and the five hunters rode down the sandy slope. Halfway down, they split up, two heading west, three heading east. Fero and two of his comrades would cut off the riders and attack. When they inevitably turned to flee, they would find their line of retreat blocked by the other two Bone Hunters. It would be over in minutes.

And Vulcanus will take only a little longer than that, thought Fero. *Let the Agori plan and prepare. Let them watch the sands for signs of our approach. They will never see us coming.*

No one ever does.

✪ F O U R ✪

After a few hours of riding, Ackar abruptly cut to the west across the riverbed. The sun was just beginning to rise behind them as they traveled over the dunes. Gelu could see the telltale marks in the sand that indicated Vorox had been through here. The further they went, the more numerous the signs. Vorox tunnels left a very unique pattern in the sand, and the two riders were surrounded by them now. Gelu moved his hand close to his launcher.

Ackar pointed to a rise up ahead, dominated by a small mountain chain. Gelu could see a cave opening about halfway up the central peak. "That's where we're going," said Ackar.

Gelu suddenly had a very bad feeling that he knew this "friend" of Ackar's. But what was with all the traces of Vorox? At first, he couldn't see any connection — a moment later he realized that he preferred it that way.

They were about 500 yards from the rocks when the Vorox appeared, erupting out of the sand all around them. Zesk, the smaller versions of the Vorox, were scattered about, too, chattering and making threatening gestures toward the two Glatorian. Gelu went for his launcher, but Ackar grabbed his wrist and kept him from reaching it.

"Do you really think you could shoot your way out of this?" Ackar said quietly. "If things go really badly, we'll charge for the cave — it's easier to defend. Until then, let me handle this." Ackar paused, then said, "Scared?"

Seconds ticked by.

"Sure," Gelu answered.

"Good. That means you aren't crazy. I don't like having crazy people watching my back."

Ackar turned toward the cave. He shouted, "Malum! I need to talk to you."

The assembled Vorox murmured among themselves and drew a little closer. One reached out to paw Gelu's sand stalker. Gelu restrained himself from taking a swipe with his blade, but the look he gave the Vorox was enough to make the savage back off.

"Malum!" Ackar called again. "Show yourself!"

The exiled Glatorian appeared in the mouth of the cave. His scarlet armor was cracked in places and caked with sand in others. Malum had always been bigger and stronger than Ackar and his time in the wastelands hadn't changed that. But Gelu was certain many other things were different now — living out in the sands would do that to a being.

"Ackar," Malum said. His voice was almost too quiet to hear. The tone was a mix of surprise and satisfaction, as if seeing his old sparring partner again was something he had been looking forward to for some time. Gelu wasn't sure if that was a good thing or a bad thing.

Malum barked a command in a language Gelu didn't understand. Instantly, the Vorox backed away three steps, but they did not put their weapons away. If anything, they seemed to have changed from merely curious about the visitors to ready for an attack. Ackar was right about one thing — the two Glatorian were surrounded, so there would be no fighting their way free.

"What brings you to my . . . empire?" Malum asked Ackar. He gestured to the sea of sand that stretched out in every direction. "If you are seeking hospitality, I have none to offer. Food? Water? Whatever I have goes to feed my people."

"Your people?" Gelu said. "You mean the Vorox? They aren't anyone's 'people.' They're just this side of sand bats."

"You're right," said Malum. "But civilized society said it had no place for me. The Vorox found me, sheltered me, and made me part of their tribe. We want nothing to do with your

47

world anymore, Ackar. But out of the friendship we once shared, I will allow you and your friend to depart with your lives . . . if you leave now."

Gelu thought that sounded like a great idea. He was no coward — far from it, he would take on anyone in a fight, from a Skrall on down. But this place reminded him a little too much of the Agori "settlements," the places for those who had spent too much time in the sun and sand and lost their minds.

"We need your help," said Ackar. "Vulcanus is in trouble."

Malum made a disgusted sound and turned back for the cave. "Go home, Ackar. Go home, while you still can."

"Vulcanus sheltered you, Malum. It fed you, supplied you with arms and armor, and treated you like a king," Ackar said, his tone blunt, but not cruel. "You owe it something."

Malum wheeled around, pointing at Ackar. His features were contorted with rage. "I owe them *nothing*! Look at me. Look at what I am reduced to. A 'king,' yes, until they drove me out . . . until they said I wasn't worthy of fighting and dying for them."

"Maybe they were right," said Ackar. "Maybe you're not worthy."

Dead silence. The Vorox edged closer. Gelu's hand returned to his launcher. Sure, he wouldn't stand a chance, but at least he would take some of the beasts down with him.

"You have a stake in this, too," Ackar continued. "They're Bone Hunters."

Gelu thought he saw Malum flinch a little. Bone Hunters were long-standing enemies of the Vorox. While the Hunters might steal from, or even kill, Agori and Glatorian for food or supplies, they would go after Vorox for pure sport. Although wild and brutal, the Vorox weren't smart enough to avoid Bone Hunter traps or fast enough to outrun their rock steeds. The best they could do was dive back underground, but the Hunters were willing to wait for them to come back to the surface. Bone Hunters were nothing if not patient.

"Tell me," said Malum.

Ackar laid out everything they knew, which wasn't much. He finished by saying there was a Bone Hunter camp to the east, most likely a place for them to prepare their attack on Vulcanus. "They're getting bolder," he said. "And if they can take out a village today, they can take out your 'kingdom' tomorrow."

Malum climbed down the mountainside in silence. As he approached the Glatorian, the Vorox parted to let him pass. "I care nothing about Vulcanus. Let it burn. But I would see the Bone Hunters burn first. What would you have us do?"

Gresh staggered into Tesara, leading his sand stalker. The animal had been just short of collapsing a few miles back, so the only way to get it to the village alive was to dismount and take it slow. He handed the reins to an Agori and headed for the arena.

The village's veteran Glatorian, Vastus, was in the middle of a practice session. He had been training nonstop since Atero had fallen. He was determined that Tesara would not meet the same fate.

He seemed surprised to see Gresh approaching. "I thought you were on your way to Vulcanus. What happened? Match get cancelled?"

"The village has bigger problems," Gresh replied. He gratefully accepted a cup of water Vastus offered. It tasted like sand and iron, but he drank it down in one gulp anyway.

"With one Glatorian to fight for them, I'm not surprised," Vastus laughed.

"Actually, it's three now. Ackar, Gelu . . . and me. I'm hoping you'll join us." Gresh explained the threat to the village of fire as rapidly as he could.

When he was done, Vastus shook his head. "It's a bluff. Don't you see? The Bone Hunters want you to think they are going after Vulcanus, so they conveniently drop a map. But what they really intend to do is hit another village — Tajun maybe, or here. I won't leave Tesara undefended . . . and your place is here, too."

"What if you're wrong?" asked Gresh.

"Then Tesara will be safe," Vastus answered. "And we'll open our gates to any refugees from Vulcanus who come our way. Listen, Gresh, the people in this village rely on us to help and protect them. We don't do that by worrying about other places and other tribes — let them worry about themselves."

"We're all on the same world," Gresh shot back. "What happens to them affects us, too."

"No. This is our world — this, right here, shrouded in vines and too close to Roxtus for my liking. We both saw Atero crumble. Well, not again, not to my village."

Gresh threw the cup on the ground. "But you're fine with it happening to someone else's," he said, walking away. "Sorry I wasted your time."

"This is a waste of time."

Tarix glanced at Kiina. It wasn't the first time she had said that. Knowing her, he was pretty sure it wouldn't be the last.

Raid on Vulcanus

The two were riding slowly across the sands, their eyes fixed on the ground around them. The two Glatorian of Tajun had been sent to investigate an Agori report that a small herd of wild rock steeds were in the area. Penned in and tamed, the animals would be valuable for trade. Left to run wild, they could cause enormous damage.

"Maybe," he answered. "We'll give it a little more time, though. It won't look good if we turn around now and then lose a few Agori to hungry steeds, right?"

"We're Glatorian," grumbled Kiina. "We're fighters — not scouts, not law enforcers, and not animal handlers. If they want me in the arena, fine. Otherwise, leave me alone."

Tarix sighed. He understood how Kiina felt. No one wanted the world as it was. And people like Kiina just wanted to get away, somewhere, anywhere. But there was no place to go. The only answer was to make the best of the world they had.

They were a good few miles outside of the

village now. It made Tarix a little nervous. With all the Bone Hunter activity around Tajun lately, he didn't like straying too far from the village. One raid and the whole place could go up in flames.

"I don't see any tracks," he admitted finally. "Maybe the Agori was wrong, or the herd has already moved on."

"Well, something came through here," Kiina answered. "Look over there."

Tarix saw what she was talking about. Off to the east, there were what looked like dark smudges on the sand. As the two Glatorian rode closer, the objects became more distinct. Both jumped off their sand stalkers and raced toward the site, launchers drawn.

Kiina knelt down to examine their find. Two Glatorian lay dead in the sand. There was no sign of their mounts, but there were tracks of sand stalkers and rock steeds all around. A broken Bone Hunter sword lay half buried in a dune nearby.

"They're from Vulcanus, but I don't know

them," she said. "This had to have happened last night. What were they doing way out here after dark?"

Tarix turned in a slow circle, checking out their surroundings. There was no sign of the Bone Hunters or anyone else. Whoever had done this was long gone.

"I don't know. But maybe someone in Vulcanus does," said Tarix. "We'll take these two back to Tajun and bury them. Then one of us better head to their village and let them know they've lost two Glatorian."

"I'll go," said Kiina. "You keep watch on the village. If there's any trouble, send someone out to bring me back."

Tarix looked toward the eastern peaks and said quietly, "You might be better off if you just keep on riding. If we get the kind of trouble I expect, one Glatorian more or less won't matter."

Kiina didn't need to ask him what he meant. All she had to do was look at the Bone Hunter blade in the sand.

⌦ F I V E ⌦

Ackar could tell the Bone Hunters were feeling confident. It wasn't that they had fires burning in their camp at night, visible for miles around. It wasn't even that they were talking and laughing among themselves, heedless of how sound carried in the desert. No, it was the strong smell wafting from their encampment that made it obvious that they did not think anyone to fear was around.

The spiky Thornax spheres fired from the launchers most Glatorian carried were not Agori-made, despite their appearance. They were, in fact, the fruit of a rare plant that grew in the deserts of Bara Magna. When allowed to ripen and grow hard, a Thornax became a powerful missile weapon, with spikes capable of tearing open armor.

Picked early in their development and boiled, Thornax could be softened enough to be eaten. The fruit was greasy and rubbery, the taste was foul, and the odor was worse. But for those who lived out in the wastelands, it was a delicacy. Bone Hunters picked Thornax in their travels and cooked it up into a particularly revolting kind of stew. It was that which Ackar smelled on the breeze.

Gelu and Malum stood on either side of him. There was no sign of any of the Vorox, but that was to be expected. Vorox did not march forth in armies. They burrowed under the ground and relied on taking enemies by surprise.

The two Glatorian had spent the day in Malum's cave, planning strategy. Now and then, Malum would start ranting about his treatment by the villagers of Vulcanus. Gelu would give Ackar a look that said, "Are we sure about this guy?" but he already knew the answer was "No."

Ackar crouched down and eyed the Bone Hunter camp. It was a cold night, even for Bara Magna, and the wind cut through his armor like a rusty blade. The long, mournful howls of dune wolves could be heard in the distance. The sounds were a summons to the pack, a signal that the hunt was about to begin.

"Everyone remember the plan?" said Ackar, rising. "We move fast, and we take out as many of them as we can."

Malum looked up sharply. "In my first week in the wastes, the Bone Hunters came down on me. They took my food, my water, and would have taken me if I had not been skilled with a blade. Any plan that involves their deaths is one I can easily remember."

"Umm, good," Ackar said. "If we can drive off some of their rock steeds, great. But the point is to make them cautious, wary, worried about more attacks later. A cautious Bone Hunter moves slowly, and that buys Vulcanus time."

At Ackar's signal, the three Glatorian moved off to take up their positions. Ten seconds later, there was a shrill whistle and the desert exploded with violence.

Vorox burrowed up out of the ground

around the Bone Hunter camp. Rock steeds reared, their scorpion tails flashing, as the bestial warriors appeared in their midst. Caught by surprise, the Bone Hunters struggled to mount a defense against the ferocious attack. The Vorox took down half a dozen Hunters in as many seconds, but the remaining formed a line and fired their Thornax launchers. The spiked missiles tore through the ranks of the Vorox, killing some and wounding many more. But the strongest effect was to make the attackers bellow with rage and surge forward again.

A few of the wiser Hunters made it to their steeds and rode out of the camp. Ackar heard one of them yell and knew he must have ridden right to where Malum was waiting in ambush. To his right, Gelu was locked in combat with a couple more Hunters who were trying to escape the Vorox attack on foot.

Ackar mounted his sand stalker and charged the line of Bone Hunter marksmen. He smashed into them from behind, scattering them like grains of sand in a storm, then wheeled around and did it again. This time, the Hunters were ready. A slash from a sword almost unseated Ackar, but he held on to the reins until he was clear of the camp.

When he turned his mount around, he saw one of the Bone Hunters darting toward the campfire and throwing something in. The next moment, the small fire erupted, turning into a white-hot blaze twenty times its original size. Under the cover of the flames, the Bone Hunters counterattacked. This time, the Vorox broke, fleeing into the desert or trying to retreat back into their tunnels. The Bone Hunters pursued, cutting them down as they fled. Malum rode in to defend his followers, fighting hard to cover their retreat.

Deciding they had done what they could here, Ackar rode to where Gelu was still strug- gling with two Hunters. He charged into the fray, knocking both Hunters to the ground, then scooped Gelu onto the back of his mount. Together, they rode from the burning campsite.

Then Gelu leapt from Ackar's sand stalker to his own, and they headed back to Malum's cave.

Malum was already there when they arrived, surrounded by the remnants of his force. Many Vorox had been lost in the fight, many more wounded, but Malum seemed satisfied. "We have dealt them a blow," he said, pride in his tone. "They will not lightly pass through our region again. Now they know the jaws of a Vorox bite deep!"

The battered Vorox raised their weapons in the air and roared. Ackar and Gelu both felt chills run through them.

"The Hunters will almost certainly come looking for revenge," said Ackar. "Maybe not now, but they won't let this go unpunished. Watch your back, Malum."

"They will not find us," the exiled Glatorian replied. "We can disappear like a single grain of sand in a vast desert."

"You're sure you won't help us defend Vulcanus?" asked Ackar. "We could use your sword."

Malum shook his head. "Those days are past. But I wish you strength in the battle to come."

"Thank you," said Ackar.

Malum turned to Gelu, reaching out to grasp the Glatorian's sword arm. "Die well, warrior."

"Right. Sure," Gelu answered, gently pulling away. "Likewise."

Ackar and Gelu rode from the camp as dawn broke over Bara Magna. Both were tired and sore, with the real fight still ahead of them. But this first skirmish had been won.

Raanu watched as Agori villagers placed rocks atop a makeshift wall along the western edge of Vulcanus. Since the discovery of the map, he had ordered all other work to be stopped and every resident to start constructing walls both inside and outside the village. What had existed up to now was enough to keep desert creatures away, but wouldn't slow down a Bone Hunters' raiding party or a Skrall attack.

He glanced at the map again. Yes, he decided, his strategy made perfect sense. The Bone Hunters would be attacking from the north and west. They could never make it through the sea of sand to the south, and treacherous Iron Canyon to the east. No sane military expedition would choose to go through its dark and winding pathways.

A cry went up from one of the villagers. Raanu looked up to see a blue-armored Glatorian riding in. He recognized Kiina immediately and went to greet her.

"You got our message, then?" he said. His smile faded at the look in her eyes.

"No," Kiina replied. She reached into her pack and tossed him a few fragments of broken weaponry. "I got your messengers. Or, rather, the Bone Hunters did. What were you thinking, sending them out in the middle of the night?"

Raanu flinched at the angry tone in her voice. Still, her reaction was no surprise. Kiina was fiercely protective of her fellow Glatorian. Villages that put them in reckless danger, or worse, didn't pay on time, could always expect to hear from her.

He hurriedly explained the situation. As he did, her expression changed from furious to concerned to grim. She dismounted and walked over to him.

"You need to leave Vulcanus. Now," she said, keeping her voice just above a whisper. "No one respects Ackar more than I do, but he's wrong. A handful of Glatorian won't stop a Bone Hunter raid. They'll just add to the body count."

Raanu turned away. Deep down, he knew she was probably right. But Gelu and Ackar had given him hope that the village could be defended. It wasn't just the loss of homes or resources he worried about. If they started running now, where would it stop?

"I've thought about that," he said, his voice flat. "But what happens when we run out of desert to hide in? The Bone Hunters will track and kill us all, and all we will have bought ourselves is a few extra weeks or months to live like cowards. I'd rather fight and die, here and now, than die by inches on the run."

"And your people? What about them?" asked Kiina, her words cracking like a whip. "What if they would prefer a chance at life, rather than certain death? Who are you to make this decision for them?"

Raanu turned to face her, his body shaking with barely contained rage. "I am the leader of this village! These people have placed their trust in me, and I will do what I think is best. I owe it to them to let them fight and die standing straight and tall like Agori, not slinking away into the night like rock jackals. If you don't want to help, get back on your animal and leave our village."

Before Kiina could answer, the muffled sound of sand stalker hoofbeats came from behind her. She drew her weapon and spun, ready for a Bone Hunter attack. To her relief, it was just Ackar and Gelu riding in. They and their mounts looked exhausted.

"We slowed them down," Gelu reported, "with a little help from Malum."

"Malum?" Raanu said. There was both surprise and contempt in his voice.

"Yeah," Gelu said, leaping down from his beast. "He's a little weird — make that, a lot weird — but he came through for you when it counted."

"It's good to see you, Kiina," said Ackar. He dismounted and handed his sand stalker off to an Agori, who would give it food and water.

"I wish I could say the same," she answered. "Why are you telling these people they can save their village? You know what Bone Hunters can do."

"Yes, I do," said Ackar. "But if we run from them, what do we do when the Skrall come? We might as well give up our weapons now, kneel down, and wait for them to take our heads off."

Ackar reached out and took her hand. "I know you don't think much of Bara Magna," he said, a little more gently. "But it's the only world we have. I'm not going to let scum like the Bone Hunters have it without a fight."

"And the fight's coming," Gelu added. "They're moving slow, probably on the lookout for more Vorox attacks, but only a couple days away at most."

"They know we have the map," said Ackar. "You would think they would come at us full speed, before we can prepare for them."

"Maybe they aren't worried about us preparing," said Gelu. "They don't think we can stop them. It wouldn't be the first time Bone Hunters were overconfident."

"They have no need to rush," Ackar observed. "Vulcanus isn't going anywhere."

"Well, if we want to keep it that way, we'd better get to work," said Gelu.

Hours passed as the Glatorian helped the Agori strengthen the village's defenses. After standing aside and watching for a while, Kiina finally shrugged her shoulders and pitched in, as Ackar knew she would. They had been friends a long time. She wouldn't let him face this alone, even if she would never admit it.

"Thanks," said Ackar. "There's no one I'd rather have beside me in a fight."

Kiina looked away, so Ackar wouldn't see her smile. In her gruffest tone, she said, "Save it. I'm only doing this because maybe the fight here will take down enough Bone Hunters and they'll leave Tajun alone for a while. Not because I think we have any hope of winning."

"Your optimism is a joy to behold," muttered Gelu.

"Riders!" shouted an Agori guard.

The three Glatorian rushed to the western walls. Gresh was on his way in, riding alongside an Iconox Glatorian named Strakk and a few others from Tesara that no one recognized. Ackar guessed they were apprentices.

Gelu pulled Gresh aside as soon as he was off his stalker. "You got Strakk to come? How did you manage that?"

"I told him Vulcanus is sitting on top of a fortune in high quality exsidian," Gresh whispered. "And that we get to divvy it up among ourselves if we beat the Bone Hunters."

"What? They haven't had exsidian in Vulcanus in fifteen thousand years at least," Gelu said. "Everyone knows that."

"Everyone but Strakk," Gresh smiled. "You know him, he won't pick up a sword unless there's a reward involved. So I let him think there was one."

"What happens when he finds out that Vulcanus is sitting on top of nothing but sand and rock?"

Gresh ran a finger along the edge of his shield, testing its sharpness. When he was satisfied, he looked at Gelu and said, "If we live long enough for that to happen . . . I'll worry about it then."

The Tesaran fighter headed for where Ackar stood with the others. Gelu followed behind. "News," Gresh said. "I met up with an Agori on the way here. He said the Skrall tipped him to the Bone Hunter's plan of attack."

"What was an Agori doing talking to Skrall?" asked Ackar, clearly skeptical.

"It was right before the Skrall raid on Atero," Gresh answered. "He was recruiting Glatorian for Raanu. After all, the village is undefended whenever you're traveling for a match, Ackar. Anyway, this Agori was nuts enough to think a Skrall would help out. What's even crazier is that the Skrall hands over a Bone Hunter battle plan — says he 'found' it."

"Sounds like a trick," said Ackar. "Even before Atero, the Skrall had no reason to help Agori."

Strakk laughed. "But they might have had a reason to hurt the Bone Hunters. Now that the Skrall are in the raiding business, aren't the Hunters competition?"

"Well, the Skrall are sneaky," he agreed. "And Strakk knows sneaky, if anyone does. What did this Agori have to say?"

Gresh picked up a stick and drew a quick map of Vulcanus and the surrounding area in the sand. On the eastern side of the circle that represented the village, he drew a series of short, sharp lines.

"They're going to attack from the east, not the north and west like we thought," he said. "They're coming through Iron Canyon."

"That's ridiculous," said Raanu. He grabbed the stick away from Gresh and added his own lines and crosses to the path Gresh had sketched out. "Stone falls, narrow twists and turns, paths so steep even a rock steed wouldn't try them . . . they would have to be insane to take that route."

Ackar crouched down and looked more closely at the map. Then he glanced to the east. The sun was at his back, its rays illuminating the jagged peaks that made up the canyon. Anyone who knew the Vulcanus region knew how treacherous Iron Canyon could be. He had once fought a month-long battle there, in the days before the disaster that rocked the entire planet. It turned into a lethal game of hide-and-find, as two armies crept though passages too narrow for more than one warrior to pass through at a time. If the leader of the column got killed, he would block the path, leaving all those behind him exposed to the spears and arrows of the enemy in pursuit.

The veteran fighter stood and walked across the village to the rim of the canyon, the other Glatorian following silently behind. He looked down at the vast expanse, still able to hear the shouts of the wounded and see the bodies of the fallen. No one who had lived through the battles of Iron Canyon could look at the place and see just piles of rock and a dried-up riverbed.

It was a killing ground.

Ackar picked up a rock and threw it into the canyon, listening to the sharp crack as it ricocheted off the face of a peak. "Attacking from this direction is ridiculous and crazy and something no sane raider would do," he said. "That's exactly why they're doing it . . . because it's the last thing we would expect."

"All our defenses face the north and west," Raanu said, a trace of fear in his voice now. "If they come from the east . . . Ackar, we have to get to work. We have to build new walls along the canyon rim, and —"

"No," said Ackar. "Leave everything as it is."

Kiina nodded her agreement. "He's right. Let them think they've surprised us."

Ackar regarded her, a small smile creeping onto his lips. "'Us'? Does that mean you're staying?"

Kiina shrugged, refusing to look at him. "Well, if you're all determined to get yourselves killed and leave me with having to spread the news, forget it. I hate playing messenger. I'd rather go out fighting and let someone else tell the tales."

Gelu scanned the canyon, then looked at Gresh. "What do you think?"

Gresh idly kicked some pebbles and watched them fall into the canyon. "I think the Bone Hunters are about to make a very big mistake," he said. "And we're going to help them make it."

* * *

Fero growled a curse at the other members of his raiding party. Since they had broken camp, Hunters kept riding off into the wastes to slay Vorox or Zesk. Ordinarily, Fero didn't mind a little recreational killing, but it was slowing down the march. Not to mention that losing the Hunters on his flanks put the rest of the squad in danger.

"Forget the beasts," he snapped. "There will be time to settle with them later."

"We waste time," one of the younger Hunters muttered. "Vulcanus has nothing we need, yet we prepare to strike it. Bone Hunters should not be a club to be wielded by another."

There was a low rumble of agreement among the ranks. It was an open secret that the decision to attack Vulcanus was not one made by the Bone Hunter leaders alone — they had been "pointed" in that direction by a helpful new ally. Fero had to admit he had his own questions about that. Who benefited the most from this raid? Were the Bone Hunters being used?

As Fero, veteran Bone Hunter, he could have these thoughts. As assigned leader of the raid, he could not allow himself to question the task — or let anyone else question it, either. He wheeled Skirmix and rode up to the young Hunter. Moving almost too swiftly for the eye to follow, he drew his blade and struck, killing the rebellious youth. Then he kicked the corpse off the back of its rock steed and watched it hit the sand with a dull thud.

Silence.

Fero looked up from the body and glanced at the faces of his raiding party, one after another. Some had glared defiance, but quickly masked the expression. Others could not meet his eyes at all.

"Anyone else with something to say?" he asked. There was cold steel in his voice.

No one answered. Satisfied, Fero returned to his place at the front of the column. "Then we ride," he said.

ⅢⅢ SIX ⅢⅢ

Seated atop his makeshift throne, Tuma
smiled.

In his time as leader of the Skrall, he had
faced victories and defeats. The years had hard-
ened him and taught him a great deal. He had
learned that a wise ruler does not waste his own
people in a war if he can trick others into doing
the fighting for him. He had also learned that
razor-sharp cunning could cut deeper than any
blade.

These past weeks had been his masterpiece
in a long career of deception, manipulation, and
conquest. First, he had managed to rein in his
Skrall warriors who wanted to raid, kill, and raze
the Agori villages from the start. Tuma counseled
patience. First, he wanted to see the strength
of the Glatorian and how unified the villages
were. He played along with the villages, dutifully

sending his Skrall to fight in the arena for things they were more than strong enough to seize.

Once he realized the villages were fractured, he carried out an experiment. He secretly helped the Bone Hunters "discover" that a trade caravan was headed for the village of Tajun. The Hunters, naturally, raided it. More such tips led to more raids, with neither the Agori nor the Bone Hunters knowing the information was coming from the Skrall. Instead of coming to the aid of Tajun, the other villages tried to profit from their misery and happily took control of resources when their Glatorian beat Tajun's in the arena. That was an important lesson — an Agori village would not go out of its way to defend another from attack.

Tuma had another weapon in his arsenal about which the villages knew nothing. One of the Agori had betrayed his people. He was feeding information to the Skrall, and then from the Skrall to the Bone Hunters. The Hunters used that information to strike where it would hurt the Agori most: their caravans and their resource-gathering sites. The result was that the Glatorian and Agori focused on the Bone Hunters as their most dangerous enemy, ignoring the real threat of the Skrall until it was too late. The fall of Atero took the Agori completely by surprise. But instead of uniting against a common foe, each village just built higher walls to protect itself. And none of them realized that their worst enemy was behind those walls, one of them.

His musings were interrupted by the arrival of Stronius. As one of the very few Skrall warriors to be honored with an actual name, Stronius commanded respect from the other residents of Roxtus. His support of Tuma's plans had helped quell any discontent among the other warriors.

"It's done," said Stronius. "The Bone Hunters' battle plans are in the hands of the Vulcanus Glatorian, as you wished. Leader . . . with all faith in your wisdom and power . . . I wonder if —"

"You wonder why I would risk Vulcanus knowing the Bone Hunters will attack from the east?" Tuma finished for him. The Skrall leader grasped his sword and rose. He towered above Stronius.

"No, I wouldn't question, only . . ." Stronius hesitated. His choice of words here might be the difference between getting an answer to a puzzle that plagued him and getting his head cut off. "Don't you want Vulcanus to fall?"

Tuma's eyes narrowed for a moment and his grip tightened on his weapon. Then, deciding that Stronius was simply asking for information, not seeking to challenge his authority, he relaxed. "Vulcanus is a test," he said. "I already know my Skrall can sack a village — they proved that in Atero. But can the Bone Hunters do the same? That is what I wish to find out. By arranging for Raanu and his people to expect the attack, I have simply made the test a little harder."

The Skrall leader smiled again, the broad, predatory grin of a sun-rock dragon. "If the Bone Hunters win, Vulcanus is eliminated as a player in this game and there are that many fewer Glatorian to oppose us. If the Hunters lose, their ranks will have been thinned and they won't be making plans of rebellion."

Tuma brushed past Stronius and headed for the exit to the courtyard. "Either way . . . as it always has been, as it always will be . . . the Skrall win."

"Squeeze," said Kiina. "Don't pull. Squeeze."

The Tajun Glatorian was standing over an Agori, who was lying on his stomach on the ground near the canyon's rim. In the Agori's hands was a Thornax launcher, the same kind used by the Glatorian. As actual Thornax were going to be needed for the coming battle, the launcher was loaded with rocks.

The target for the budding marksman was a small pile of rocks atop a nearby peak. So far, he'd had a hard time just hitting the mountain, let alone anything *on* the mountain. This time, though, he was sure he would do it. He yanked back on the trigger, the weapon jerked up in the air, and the rock went flying . . . straight up. Kiina pulled him out of the way before his shot could come back down and smack him on the head.

"I said, squeeze!" snapped Kiina. "You're not ripping a fireroot out of the ground. When the Bone Hunters come through, every shot is going to count."

"I know," said the Agori. "I'm sorry. I just . . . I don't know how to fight."

Kiina's tone softened. "I know. Must be nice."

She reached down and gently took the launcher away from him. "Can you use a knife? Go talk to Gresh. He's going to need people to cut the vines at the right moment."

The Agori smiled, scrambled to his feet, and hurried off. Kiina watched him go. The Agori as a whole had a lot of enthusiasm for this fight. Had it really been so long that they no longer remembered what war was like? She wondered how many sunrises some Vulcanus villagers had left to see.

Forcing the thought from her mind, she

handed the launcher off to the next Agori in line. "Now, *squeeze* the control. Understand?"

Not far away, Gresh was hard at work with his own team of Agori. They had been doing hard labor all day, hauling up rocks from the floor of the canyon to the slopes. Each rock was placed inside a net made of fireroot vine, which was stretched between two peaks. In addition to being flameproof, fireroot was incredibly strong, so the net could hold tons of stone.

The trap itself was simple. When the Bone Hunters rode through this part of the canyon, an Agori would cut the vines so that the rocks would fall on the invaders far below. There were two things that made the execution of the plan tricky. The first was timing — cut the vine too early or too late, and the rocks would miss. The second was that fireroot could be extremely difficult to cut. The villager on watch would have only a few seconds to slice through it.

"It's all in the wrist," said Gresh, demonstrating on a spare piece of vine. He flicked his dagger and cut through the thick tendril easily. "Now you try."

Metus gave Gresh an uncertain glance and then took the knife from him. The Agori did his best to duplicate the Glatorian's move, but the blade got stuck halfway through the vine. Metus tried to wrestle it free, but couldn't. Standing off to the side waiting for his turn, Raanu couldn't help laughing. Metus shot him a glare.

"If you want more fighters for your arena, you'll knock it off," Metus growled.

"Oh, relax," smiled Raanu. "You ice tribe sorts are used to breaking icicles, not anything that requires real muscle."

The leader of Vulcanus took the knife from Metus's hand and severed the fireroot in one clean stroke. "See? Easy."

"Yeah. Right," Metus answered. "Think I'll go find somebody a little more my style to work with, like Gelu or Strakk." The Agori paused, looking around. "Hey . . . where is Strakk, anyway?"

*　　*　　*

For the sixth time in the last hour, Ackar sur-
veyed the canyon. The Glatorian and Agori had
done their work well. Rock falls were set up in
numerous places, some controlled from up
above, some connected to trip wires. And if the
Hunters made it to the village, well, there would
be a few surprises waiting for them there
as well.

Ackar had planned as best he could, but he
couldn't escape the feeling that he had missed
something. This kind of doubt was nothing new
for him. As he grew older, he found winning in
the arena was getting more difficult. He tired a
little more easily and it took longer to recover
from injuries. Younger, stronger fighters were
pushing him to his limit in matches.

It was only natural, he supposed. He had
been fighting in the arena for many years. Time,
they said, was the only enemy a Glatorian couldn't
beat. Eventually, even the best fighter would lose
a little bit off his speed and his reflexes, maybe
lose a little power behind his blows. One day, he

would be beating anyone who challenged him. The next, he could be losing to backstabbing little creeps like Strakk. And the day after that, his village wouldn't need him anymore. If he were lucky, they would run him out for unimportant fights. If he wasn't, he'd become a wanderer, hiring his sword out for a hot meal or a place to sleep.

Ackar was determined that would not happen to him. He'd rather die in battle with the Bone Hunters than end up pitied by another Glatorian. He refused to wind up like Malum — *I'm old, but not crazy*, he reminded himself.

Weapon in hand, he headed back to the central shelter in the village. It was time to hone his blade to a razor-sharp edge. Perhaps that would make up for the edge he was no longer certain he had.

That night, the four Glatorian — Gelu, Gresh, Kiina, and Ackar — and Raanu sat around a table in the shelter. They had finished their evening meal and talk had quieted down. They had gone over the plan so often that Kiina was sure she would be reciting it in her sleep.

Strakk's absence worried Gresh more than he wanted to admit. He had been responsible for bringing the Iconox fighter to Vulcanus. He didn't know Strakk all that well, having only traveled the desert with him a time or two, but he knew some of the stories about him weren't pleasant. Strakk was good in a fight, that was true, but he was also all about profit. If the Bone Hunters offered him a better price than he thought he might get for Vulcanus' "treasure," would he sell out the village? It bothered Gresh that he didn't know the answer to that question.

Outside, sharp-eyed villagers kept watch on the canyon. Fires had been doused in the village so the light would not outline the figures of the Agori and give their positions away. No one spoke or made a noise of any kind. Every sentry clutched his weapon and waited for the sound of rock steeds galloping across the sand.

"Tomorrow, you think, then?" Raanu asked, for the third time.

"If not tonight," replied Ackar. His tone was surprisingly gentle. He understood why Raanu was so anxious. They were all tense. Snapping at the village leader would achieve nothing.

"They should have been here by now," Gelu said. "Unless that fight with the Vorox really rattled them. If it were anyone other than Bone Hunters, I would think they had turned back and gone home."

Kiina chuckled. "If they went back empty-handed, it would be the last trip they ever made."

"They're coming," Ackar said firmly. "Bone Hunters finish what they start."

Raanu swallowed hard. Now that the fight was almost here, he was having doubts. What if the plan failed? What if the Glatorian fled, leaving the villagers to the mercy of the Bone Hunters? Maybe fighting wasn't the best idea, after all.

"Listen," Raanu said, his eyes fixed on the

floor. "The Bone Hunters just want to steal from us, like they have done before. They will ride in, take our food and anything else of value, and leave. If we stay out of their way, no one gets hurt. But if we try to fight . . . they could kill us all."

"They could," agreed Ackar.

"And burn the village to the ground," said Raanu.

"Most likely," answered Ackar.

There was a long silence. Raanu never lifted his eyes to meet Ackar's gaze.

"Do you want us to leave?" Ackar asked finally. "We can grab our weapons and ride out tonight. You can leave the traps alone and just let the Bone Hunters ride in . . . if that's what you really want."

Raanu shifted uncomfortably in his chair. "It's not . . . but I have to think of my people. If all the Hunters want are food and supplies . . ."

"That's not all they want." The voice belonged to Strakk, who was standing in the doorway, smiling. He advanced a step into the room and kicked the door shut behind him. "Not by a long shot."

The assembled Glatorian looked at him; some surprised, some angry. Strakk glanced at each of them, his grin growing broader. Then he returned his attention to Raanu. "Listen, little Agori. The Bone Hunters don't want your scraps of food, your cobbled-together tools, or your patchwork weapons. They want your lives."

Ackar shot up, furious. "If you know something, Strakk, say it. Otherwise, get out."

Strakk sat down, propping his feet up on the table. Kiina knocked them off with a swipe of her armored hand.

"I've had a long day," she said. "Don't make it longer."

"Well, it's like this," said Strakk, sounding very satisfied with himself. "This afternoon, I decided to go out scouting for the Bone Hunters . . . you know, get an idea of how close they were, how many, that sort of thing."

Gelu looked at Strakk in disbelief. Then he

shook his head and said to the others, "He was running away."

Strakk ignored the jibe. "So there I was, riding along, and I spot the Bone Hunters just up ahead. I figured, great opportunity, so I snuck closer to try and hear what they were saying. Naturally, they didn't see me — no one does, unless I want to be seen."

Gelu snorted. "He was hiding. He's good at that."

This time, Strakk shot him a nasty look, as if challenging Gelu to say something else. Then he went on with his story. "As I was saying . . . I overheard them talking. They didn't say anything about looting Vulcanus. They talked about wiping it off the map."

Raanu stiffened, but whether with fear or new resolve, no one present could tell.

"Naturally, when I heard that, I rode back here to warn you all," Strakk finished.

"The Bone Hunters were between him and Iconox," said Gelu. "So he had to turn around and come back."

Strakk leapt up, weapon in hand, and kicked his chair across the room. Gelu got up, too, ready to fight. Kiina got between them before a blow could be landed. "Only if you want to dance with me first," she said to Strakk. The look in her eyes acted like a bucket of cold water on Strakk's hot temper, and he backed off a step.

Kiina glanced over her shoulder at Gelu. "Sit down. We don't have time for this."

Gelu shrugged and walked away. Kiina gave Strakk a little shove toward the opposite side of the room. "It sounds like we have enough people that want to kill us," she said, "without us doing it to each other."

"That's it, then," said Gresh. "Now we know what we're up against."

"Raanu? It's your village," said Ackar. "Your call. Fight or run?"

"They want to kill us," Raanu said softly. "We, who have never harmed them . . . all we've tried to do is live our lives and make it through each day. And if they win here, this will just be the start."

He rose and looked Ackar right in the eye. "No. We fight. With you or without you, we fight."

Ackar nodded. Then he turned to his fellow Glatorian. "All right, then. Any of you who wants to leave, now's the time. No one will think any less of you."

Kiina gave Strakk a hard look, saying, "Don't even think about it."

"I'm in," said Gresh. "If the Agori want my help, I won't walk away."

All eyes turned to Gelu then. Defending the village had been his suggestion in the first place, but now he felt his mouth go dry and his gut grow cold. What Strakk had revealed meant almost certain death for anyone who stayed in Vulcanus.

But Gelu also knew Ackar was wrong about one thing: the other Glatorian *would* think less of anyone who left. Even if none of them lived long, they would go to their graves thinking that he was a coward if he fled. Gelu was afraid, but he was no coward.

"Sure, why not?" he said, trying to sound casual about the whole thing. "I don't have anything planned for this week anyhow."

Ackar turned to the Glatorian from Tajun. "Kiina?"

"This is completely crazy, you know that," Kiina said.

"Completely," Ackar agreed.

"It's not like the Agori are suddenly going to look at us like we're heroes," she continued. "We'll still be just the hired help to them."

"Most likely," Ackar said, nodding.

"Best we're going to do is slow the Bone Hunters down a little . . . maybe give them something to think about the next time."

"That's probably the best we'll do," said Ackar. "Are you in or out?"

Kiina gave him a long look. "We've fought in the arena how many times, Ackar? Sometimes I win, sometimes you win. I want to make sure I get another chance to knock you down in the arena. I'm in."

That left Strakk. He looked around the

room, being careful to avoid Kiina's gaze. "I've done a lot," he said. "Without me, you would think they were just coming here to raid you. Anyway, I was thinking I might be of more use riding out to find reinforcements. Of course, I'd like to stay with you —"

"Good," Ackar cut him off. "Then you will."

He turned to the others. "Get some rest. I want everyone in position before dawn. Let's give those Bone Hunters a fight they'll remember."

⚋ S E V E N ⚋

Fero led his Bone Hunters into Iron Canyon. "Be watchful," he ordered. "This place is more treacherous than a sun serpent."

The unspoken question among the other Hunters was why they were there at all. The question was valid — but after what happened to the last of their number who talked out of turn no one would ask it again. Fero knew that they could have just ridden in from the west, across open desert, and overwhelmed any Agori defenses they encountered. But that wasn't the point.

The Agori were already on edge after what happened to Atero. Once Vulcanus fell, they would panic. Trade would drop to nothing. New walls would go up everywhere. Arena matches would stop as each village armed its Glatorian and used them for defense. Raids would get more difficult and more costly. That meant Bone Hunters had to get used to doing things the hard way, with a little more strategy and a little less charging across the sand right at the enemy.

As they rode single file along the narrow trails, Fero scanned the peaks on both sides, looking for traps. He saw no sign of any new defenses. The first rays of morning sun did not reflect off the armor or weapons of warriors hidden among the rocks. It was just as he expected. The Agori would never dream of anyone attacking from this maze of rock.

Let the hunt begin, thought Fero.

Despite his keen eyes, Fero had indeed missed something. Hidden high among the peaks was a single Agori from Vulcanus. The villager's own eyes widened as he saw the column of Bone Hunters entering the canyon. He hadn't really believed until this moment that they were truly planning to invade his village. Now that they were here, he knew what to do.

He cupped his mouth with his hands and made the cry of a sand bat. The cry would be picked up and carried along the line of Agori watchpoints until the message was received in Vulcanus itself. The meaning of it was simple: the Bone Hunters are coming.

The mock creature cry set off a flurry of activity in the village. Agori grabbed their tools and took up their stations around and inside their shelters. Ackar, Strakk, and Kiina readied themselves for the fight that was to come.

"It's all up to Gresh and Gelu now," said Ackar.

"Why doesn't that fill me with confidence?" Strakk muttered.

"You just better hope the Bone Hunters don't fill you with Thornax," Kiina said, smiling.

"And ruin my good looks?" Strakk replied. "They wouldn't dare."

Fero heard the repeated sand bat cries, each one farther away than the one before. He slowed

Skirmix to a walk, and listened. There were no other sounds. He frowned, troubled.

One sand bat in a place like Iron Canyon was no great surprise, but four or five? Impossible. With its voracious appetite, a lone sand bat could decimate the wildlife in a region. For that reason, two or more sand bats never lived anywhere close to each other.

Something was wrong.

"Eyes on the rocks," he barked. "If anything moves, kill it."

The three dozen Bone Hunters that traveled with Fero immediately began sweeping their eyes up the slopes on both sides of the trail. Too late, one spotted the glint of a dagger high among the rocks, to the left and just behind the column. Before the Bone Hunter could fire his Thornax launcher, the Agori villager took his knife and sliced through a fireroot vine. The next moment, a half ton of rock rolled down the slope, sealing the canyon exit.

The rock steeds hissed and reared up in surprise. Clouds of stone dust billowed forth, blinding and choking the Bone Hunters. Fero cursed and ordered his men to get their mounts under control and get moving.

Up above, his job done, the Agori scrambled across the peaks and headed for his next post. By the time the dust cleared enough for the Bone Hunters to take a shot at him, he was already out of range.

Fero wheeled Skirmix to look at the damage. Their way back out of the canyon was now fully blocked. There was no choice but to go forward, into the village of Vulcanus. He had no illusions what that meant. The Agori would not be trying to drive his squad forward unless there were more traps waiting further along.

Very well then, he thought. *We will march through their petty snares and right into their village. And when we leave it, there won't be two stones left standing together.*

Up ahead, Gelu made ready for the Bone Hunters' arrival. His trap was modeled after something the Iconox villagers had used for years to stop marauding mountain worms. Granted, there it was carved from ice and made over the course of weeks, and here it was wood, rock, and fire-root slapped together. But he had faith the effect would be the same.

It was a simple device. Four long shafts of wood were laid out on the ground, then two more laid across them to form a latticework. Fireroot was used to lash them together. Pieces of volcanic rock sharpened to a point were then fitted into each of the joints. Finally, the whole construct was hauled up the side of a peak and tied to the rock with vine. When the vine was cut . . . things would get interesting.

Of course, if it didn't work, it was doubtful Gelu would live long enough to worry about it. It was funny — even in his time as a paid guard for caravans, he had never really thought about the possibility of dying. There had been some tough fights out in the desert, but somehow he knew he would always survive. This time, he wasn't so sure.

That doubt sharpened his mind a great

deal. Everything felt much more intense to him. The vivid, dark orange of the rock all around him; the icy feel of the weapon in his hand; the soft sounds of insects skittering among the stones; the scent of fireroot and ash . . . every color was bright, every sound magnified, every aroma almost overpowering.

It made him wonder. Malum's life was at risk every moment — you couldn't exist out in the wastelands without a constant awareness that death was riding beside you. Was this how he felt, then? And if so, was it any surprise he was a little . . . crazy? Gelu couldn't imagine what it would be like to have every sight, sound, and sensation be magnified all the time.

Right now, though, his enhanced senses were a blessing. He could hear the distinctive sound of rock steeds moving along the trail. A moment later, he could see Fero at the head of the column. Now came the hard part. He had to be patient.

Gelu waited as, down below, Fero rode by. Then another Bone Hunter, and another, until about half a dozen had made it past Gelu's hiding place. This was the moment. Gelu slashed the fireroot, and the latticework fell. It crashed atop the middle of the column, knocking Bone Hunters from their steeds. Even from his perch high above, Gelu could tell at least a few Bone Hunters wouldn't be getting back up again.

A Thornax struck the rock near him and exploded, showering him with shards of stone. He looked down to see it had been fired by Fero. The lead Bone Hunter was pointing up at his hiding place and shouting. Temporarily deafened by the Thornax blast, Gelu couldn't hear what his old enemy was saying, but he could guess. It was time to get out of here, he thought.

Down below, Bone Hunters were working to help their felled comrades by hacking the latticework to pieces. More had joined Fero in firing up at the rocks. Gelu, staying low, scrambled across the peaks, heading back to Vulcanus. Thornax blew the rocks apart behind him as he ran. One stumble and it would be him getting blasted to pieces.

Gelu was almost to safety now, but he couldn't resist stopping to look back. He had survived, after all, and he couldn't keep the grin off his face. Looking down at Fero, he waved.

"Welcome to Vulcanus, Bone Hunter!" he shouted. Then Gelu was gone among the peaks.

So far, so good, thought Ackar. *But we have a long way to go.*

The early reports from the Agori and Gelu told the tale: the Bone Hunters had been caught by surprise, and the various traps and obstacles were slowing them down and bleeding their forces. They would still have numbers on their side when they hit Vulcanus, but they had decreased their advantage.

"What do you think?" asked Kiina.

"I think," Ackar replied, "that I wouldn't want to be Fero right now."

*   *   *

As it happened, Fero didn't want to be Fero now either. He had lost three Hunters to Gelu's trap and two more to spears thrown from up above by Agori. His men had managed to wound more than a few of the villagers, but the rest had gotten away. Fero sent up another four Hunters into the rocks to scout for traps up ahead. He saw them surprise a group of Agori waiting in ambush — none of the Agori escaped alive. The Hunters moved on, but then never came back. Fero thought he caught a glimpse of Gresh up among the peaks, which might well explain his missing men.

The anger in the ranks was about to boil over, and Vulcanus was still a long way off. If they kept on, his ranks would be bled dry by the time they reached the village. He had no doubt that he could take the place even with a reduced force, but it would be more difficult, especially since he had no idea how many Glatorian were waiting inside.

A crude shaft flew from somewhere high up and to the left, striking one of the Bone

Hunters' rock steeds. The beast reared, hissed, and then hit the ground, pinning its rider underneath it. Others helped free him, but his leg was badly injured.

Fero made a decision. "Ready your launchers," he said. "We are turning back. We'll blow apart the obstacle at the canyon mouth and make for the desert."

"Giving up?" growled one Bone Hunter. "Bowing to Agori? Never!"

Fero raised his launcher and gestured toward the spiked orb loaded into it. "You are new to the ways of the warrior," he said, his voice flat but with anger in his eyes. "So you do not know what this can do to a body when used by a master. Do you care to find out?"

The resistant Bone Hunter promptly shut his mouth.

"We ride," said Fero. "Go!"

From his vantage point high above the trail, Gresh could not believe his eyes. The column of Bone Hunters had reversed direction and was heading out of the canyon. Had they abandoned the attack?

He turned to the two Agori with him. They were manning a net filled with rocks, waiting for the chance to unleash its contents on the invaders. "Stay here," he said. "Keep your eyes open. This could be a trick."

Staying low, Gresh scrambled over the rocks, trying to keep the column in sight. When they reached the rockfall that blocked the exit from the canyon, they blasted it apart with explosive Thornax. When the smoke and dust cleared, the Bone Hunters were gone.

But to where? That was the question.

There was only one thing to do: head back to Vulcanus, get his sand stalker, and try to find them.

When Gresh returned with the news of what he had seen, no one believed it. "When Bone Hunters do you a favor, that's the time to draw your sword," Kiina said. "They're up to something."

Ackar agreed with her, but added, "I know something about what Iron Canyon can do to you. Maybe they decided Vulcanus wasn't worth the price they would pay. But . . . we need to make sure."

Gresh, already mounted, said, "I'll be back." Then he rode out of the village.

Raanu looked at the Glatorian with hopeful eyes. "Do you think . . . they really gave up?"

"Sure," Strakk answered. "I also think rock steeds can fly."

"I'd call it unlikely," said Ackar.

"I'd call it something more colorful," said Kiina. "If you think they turned tail and ran, I have a few miles of wasteland I'd like to sell you. The Bone Hunters are up to something."

Gresh was gone for hours. During that time, Strakk picked a fight with Vulcanus's chief cook and wound up trashing the inn. Kiina stepped in to stop him, and the two wound up in a fight which did even more damage. It took Ackar and a dozen Agori to pull them apart. Raanu was not happy.

The villagers were starting to grumble as well. Glatorian were known for their healthy appetites. No one complained too much about feeding ones employed by their village, but taking food and water to give to fighters from Tesara, Tajun, and Iconox did not go over well. Even the fact that those Glatorian were there to defend the village didn't help, especially once word spread that the Bone Hunters had already fled.

Gresh rode back in after dark. He looked puzzled. "I followed them for miles. They're headed on a straight line north for the Skrall River. They were riding hard and no one broke off from the column." He shrugged. "I don't get it."

"I do," said Raanu, smiling. "They ran into more trouble than they expected here. They didn't think we would fight back. Now they'll look for someplace easier to raid."

The leader of Vulcanus walked up to Gresh

and shook his hand. Then he did the same to Kiina and, after some hesitation, Strakk as well. "You did it. You have the gratitude of every Agori in this village. We wish you a safe journey home."

"That's nice," said Strakk. "When do we get paid?"

"Raanu, we should talk about this," said Ackar. "If the Bone Hunters should come back —"

"They aren't coming back," Raanu said, in a tone that said he had no interest in an argument. "It's over. We're very grateful for the help, but Vulcanus will be all right now."

Kiina picked up her weapon and headed for the inn's exit. "If that's how you feel, so be it."

"Kiina!" Ackar called after her.

"Save it," the female Glatorian replied. "We're only good enough to risk our lives when Agori are in trouble, remember? After that, they'd rather not have us around."

"I have better things to do anyway," Gelu said, glaring at Raanu, "than stand around helping people who don't want my help. I'll collect what I'm owed before I leave, Raanu. Oh, and next time your village is in trouble — try and find me." Then he, too, was gone.

Gresh had his eyes fixed on the ground. When he spoke, his voice was tight and strained as he tried to contain his anger. "With due respect, Raanu, you're making a mistake. There has to be more to this than what we're seeing. There has to be."

"You followed them yourself," Raanu said. "You saw them go. Now it's time for you and your friends to do the same."

Without saying a word, Gresh gathered his things and left. Strakk watched him go, but made no move to leave himself. He waited until he heard the sound of Kiina, Gresh, and Gelu riding out before turning to Raanu.

"Okay, now that those three losers are gone," Strakk said, "when do we get paid?"

❇ E I G H T ❇

The next day dawned bright and clear over the village of Vulcanus. Agori were back at work, some repairing the damage Strakk had caused in the inn, others gathering food or repairing equipment. Requests to take the stones from the western walls for use elsewhere had been turned down by Raanu. The immediate threat might be over, he reasoned, but the Skrall were still out there.

"Hopefully, word will get back to the Skrall about how we treated the Bone Hunters," he said. "Then maybe they will leave us alone, too."

Raanu had little time to spend on such things, however. Metus was getting ready to ride out and the Vulcanus leader had to talk to him before he did. Metus had been expecting the discussion.

"We need more Glatorian," Raanu said. "With Malum gone, all we have is Ackar . . . and how much longer can he fight every battle on his own before he starts to lose?"

"You had Glatorian here — Gelu, Kiina, Strakk, Gresh — why not hire one of them?" asked Metus.

"Gelu no longer fights in the arena," Raanu replied. "The others have been fighting for their villages for years. They're mostly top-rank Glatorian. You know how hard it is to get someone like that to fight full-time for another village. No, we need a new fighter, one who battles and wins for Vulcanus alone."

"I found you new Glatorian," Metus replied, never slowing as he packed his vehicle with supplies. "You decided to use them as messengers to Tajun and got them killed. That's not my fault. If you are going to waste prime material that way, you can't blame me if no one wants to fight for you."

"We'll pay double," said Raanu.

Metus looked around. "You don't *have* double," he snorted.

"We need at least one more," Raanu said, a note of pleading entering his voice. "We'll slip you a little extra finder's fee."

Metus nodded. "All right. And I get to promote an Ackar-Strakk match? After what happened in the inn, I think a lot of Vulcanus Agori wouldn't mind seeing Strakk lose."

"Agreed."

"Then I'll do what I can." Metus climbed into his vehicle. "One thing, though — if I do find you someone, try not to get him killed so quickly and in such a stupid way, all right?"

Before Raanu could reply, Metus was on his way out of the village.

Not far away, Ackar watched the trainer depart. Metus had a job to do, just like any Agori, but Ackar had seen a few too many rookie fighters pushed into the ring over the years, only to get chopped down by a stronger, more experienced opponent. Some of that — maybe a lot of it — was the result of pressure from village leaders like Raanu. But Metus should have been looking out for his fighters, too.

Maybe Kiina's right, he thought. *Maybe no one looks out for the Glatorian but us.*

He looked out toward the desert. The idea that the Bone Hunters left just like that gnawed at him. Sure, the village's defenses were effective, but the Hunters had not even encountered the nastiest of them yet. It wasn't like Fero to lose his nerve.

Still, there was no sign of them. He even posted Agori to keep watch on the canyon, but nothing. Despite that, he was still angry with Raanu over his hasty decision to send the others away. He knew that was a mistake, even if all the evidence showed there was no more danger.

The day passed. When night fell, the Agori lit their torches to keep Vorox away from the village. Ackar sent a few extra villagers to keep watch for any suspicious activity in the desert. He gave up on the idea of getting any sleep himself. If something happened, he wanted to be armed and ready for it.

It was a quiet night. Agori talked among themselves in hushed tones. There was something about the dark that made everyone feel they had to keep quiet. It was almost instinctive, as if making too much noise might attract monsters that waited in the darkness.

If you asked the Vulcanus Agori Kyry, he would have told you he didn't believe in fear. He also didn't think dousing three torches in a row would mean a Vorox attack, or that stepping on a beetle mound would mean a year of bad luck. That sort of superstition was fine for some villagers, but not for him. Those fears did nothing but hold Agori back, making them too afraid to venture out of their villages and explore. For every trader or traveler, there were six other villagers who would never venture beyond the bounds of their own villages. That was not the life for him. He had done a little exploring of this world, and planned to do more.

Right now, though, his job was to keep watch on the Sea of Liquid Sand to the southwest. That was like watching metal rust. While there were a few safe paths through the area, most of it was quicksand that could swallow rock steeds in a matter of moments. Even the Vorox avoided that area.

A sound came from out in the night, so soft that he first thought he was just imagining it. It was the clink of metal on metal. Kyry froze, listening hard. Maybe it had just been the echo of a noise from inside the village.

He didn't hear anything now, only the wind swirling through the sand. Or was that the wind? It sounded like a hiss. Could it be some desert snake venturing close to the village, drawn by the heat of the torches? No, it was too low for that.

Kyry glanced up at the torch that burned beside him. Its light illuminated the area ten feet in front of him, but also made him blind to anything that might be out in the desert beyond that point. If he doused it, his eyes might adjust to the darkness, allowing him to see anything moving out in the night. On the other hand, if it was a Vorox out there, it would charge the second the flame was gone.

Now there was another sound, louder than the first two. This one made Kyry stand up and immediately douse the torch.

It was the sound of a Thornax launcher being loaded.

Bone Hunters! The words exploded in his mind. He turned to shout a warning to the village.

A strong hand clamped itself over his mouth. Kyry was yanked off his feet and hauled up onto the back of a rock steed. A single blow knocked him unconscious.

The Bone Hunters spread out into a line along the border between Vulcanus and the Sea of Liquid Sand. They were hungry and tired, but it didn't matter. All that was important was this village and the destruction they were about to wreak upon it.

Fero savored the moment. He had waited until he was certain they were not being followed to order a change in course, away from the high desert and south toward the Sea of Liquid Sand. The order caught even his own Hunters by surprise. They traveled through the wasteland between Tajun and Vulcanus, staying far from known trade routes. When they reached the treacherous Sea, they kept on for miles before looping back north. They would hit Vulcanus from a direction no one would expect.

"Attack!" Fero shouted.

The Bone Hunters struck Vulcanus like a sandstorm. Agori poured out of their shelters only to be struck down or trampled by the riders. Ackar charged into the center of the village and spotted Fero, torch in hand, lighting up one of the Agori huts. With a bellow of rage, the Glatorian rushed forward, knocking the Bone Hunter off his rock steed with one mighty blow.

Fero hit the sand hard. Ackar moved in to finish him off, but the Bone Hunter rolled away and sprang to his feet. "Look around, Glatorian," he said, gesturing to the chaos in the village. "In a matter of minutes, this village will be in ashes. You thought you could drive us off by throwing rocks? Next time, you'll know better. . . ."

Nearby, three Agori managed to unseat a Bone Hunter from his steed, but it was too late. Bone Hunters were rampaging through the village, taking whatever they could carry and smashing any resistance. It was a scene out of a nightmare, or worse, out of a memory.

"You've seen this before," said Fero. "Been part of it, too, during the battles of long past. How many villages did you see destroyed? But I can afford to show mercy. I want all of Bara Magna to know what happened here. Ride out, Ackar, and tell the tale wherever you go."

Ackar looked around. Tell the tale? A tale of failure, of death, of a village lost, and all for the greater glory of a murdering band of Bone Hunters?

"Never," Ackar answered. "The only story coming out of this night will be the one about your death."

Fero raised his sword. "Your allies are

gone. Your Agori are fleeing or dead. It's over, Ackar. You're all alone."

The Bone Hunter raised his blade to make its fatal strike. The next instant, the sword exploded into a thousand shards of metal. Fero cried out and dropped the now useless weapon.

"Don't you know by now? Glatorian have to stand together."

Fero and Ackar both turned at the sound. It was Kiina, Thornax launcher in hand, flanked by Gresh, Gelu, Strakk, Vastus, and Tarix.

"After all, if we don't, who else will?" Kiina glanced at the fighters on either side of her. Then she turned back to Fero, a fierce smile on her lips. "Let's take them."

The six Glatorian rode in hard, catching the other Bone Hunters by surprise. Fero grabbed onto his rock steed and mounted, shouting orders to his bandits to regroup. Tarix rode up to Ackar, with the Vulcanus Glatorian's sand stalker right behind him. Ackar wasted no time in mounting his beast.

"I couldn't let Kiina have all the fun," said

Tarix. "Vastus took some convincing, but the chance to bash Bone Hunters is too good to miss."

"And now we are seven," Ackar replied. "Time to hunt the Hunters."

Kyry woke up in the sand. He raised his head at the sound of shouts and Thornax exploding all around. The sight he saw was one he would never forget.

Seven Glatorian were locked in battle with three times as many Bone Hunters. Swords flashed, axes flew, and launchers fired as the two sides fought to the death. Near the border of the village, Kiina caught two Hunter swords on her trident, shoved them back, then swept both of her foes off their steeds with one swing. Both rock steeds hissed and went at her with their jaws snapping. It was the last move either would ever make.

Not far away, Gresh had his back to the wall, with four Hunters closing in. He was using his shield to parry their blows, but Kyry knew one blow would get through eventually. One Bone Hunter saw an opening and moved to attack, only to freeze in mid-strike and fall over. As he hit the ground, Kyry saw Vastus standing behind him, with a paralyzing venom spear in hand.

"Four to one? Didn't I teach you better than that?" Vastus said to Gresh. "It's not a fair fight unless it's at least six to one."

"I'll try to remember that," Gresh said, smiling, as he waded into the remaining Bone Hunters.

Gelu and Strakk fought back to back, fighting off waves of Bone Hunters. Gelu glanced over his shoulder to spot Strakk looting one of the fallen enemies. "Would you save that until the battle is over?" he snapped.

"By then, all the good loot will be gone," Strakk answered, fending off a Bone Hunter's blade with his axe. "Agori are quick, and they have sticky fingers."

"You're hopeless," said Gelu.

"I know," Strakk replied. "It's my best quality."

In the center of the village, Ackar faced Fero. The two had been fighting an even match, but now Fero could see that Ackar was starting to grow tired.

"You should have retired long ago," the Bone Hunter said mockingly. "Put down your sword and go live in the wastes with Malum. He has the right idea: to hide in the desert and hope the storm passes him."

"You Bone Hunters aren't a storm, Fero. You're not even a stiff breeze."

Ackar swung his sword. Fero blocked with his launcher. "You and your Glatorian may win this battle, but it's your last fight, Ackar. You and I both know you're past it. Why don't you just surrender?"

"Glatorian rules," Ackar smiled. "We don't get paid for losing to mindless creatures or Bone Hunters."

Fero snarled and fired his launcher. Ackar

tried to dodge, but the Thornax caught his sword arm, tearing open his armor. Fero took aim for a second shot.

A ragged scream distracted the Bone Hunter leader. He glanced to his left to see the last of his raiders fall before Kiina's trident. Now it was his turn to be all alone.

Fero had not survived in the wastes all this time by being stupid. He backed away from Ackar and grabbed the reins of his rock steed. Mounting it in one swift motion, he said, "Bone Hunters are like grains of sand in the desert — the wind may blow a few away, but there are always more to take their place. We'll meet again, Ackar."

The Glatorian tried to stop him, but his own fatigue and the pain in his wounded arm slowed him down. Fero rode out of the village and vanished into the darkness.

"Are you all right?" Kiina said, jumping down from her sand stalker.

"I'm okay," Ackar replied. "But Fero got away."

"He won't be gone long," said Gelu. "One of us will run into him and finish the job you started."

Raanu rushed over. He had been wounded, but it didn't look too serious. He shouted orders to a few other Agori to look after villagers who were more injured. Then he turned to look up at Kiina. "Why did you come back?" he asked.

"We figured the Bone Hunters would," she answered. "And if you wouldn't let us wait for them in the village, well, we decided to wait for them out there."

Raanu nodded, solemnly. "You saved us. You've done a great thing for Vulcanus."

Kiina shook her head. "You don't understand. We first came here to help you protect your village." She gestured to Ackar, "But we came back to protect him."

Kyry stumbled into the village at just that moment. He looked at the assembled Glatorian with wonder and pride. His village was damaged, his people hurt . . . but damage could be repaired, and wounds could be healed. Eventually, the pain would be forgotten.

But this victory never would be, he vowed. He would leave this village and he would spread this tale. As long as there were Agori on Bara Magna, he would make sure they knew what happened in Vulcanus. And then, maybe, they would see Glatorian as more than just swords hired for pay. They would see them as heroes.

⟨⟨ EPILOGUE ⟩⟩

Metus steered his wagon across the desert sands, still marveling at what he had just heard. He had been certain that Vulcanus would be destroyed by the Bone Hunters, and that everyone in it would be killed. How so few Glatorian managed to stop a marauding band of raiders and save the village, he did not know. But the Vulcanus Agori he had run into — a youth named Kyry — assured him it was so.

Some things had changed since the events at Vulcanus, some had not. The Bone Hunters had been badly mauled, and their raids had become less frequent. No one doubted they were out in the desert somewhere, plotting their revenge. Gelu figured that if they hit another village, it would be in much greater numbers to prevent a repeat of Vulcanus. The Glatorian hoped it would take the Bone Hunters a good, long while to assemble that big a force.

Of course, that still left the Skrall to worry about. Since the fall of Atero, they had not mounted any major attacks, but everyone knew it was just a matter of time. There had been plenty of raids by small Skrall squads, mainly to steal resources and capture Glatorian. What they were doing with the fighters they grabbed, no one seemed to know.

The loss of so many fighters was bad for the villages, but good for Metus. There was a bigger need to recruit more fighters, and it meant that the ones he managed could get higher pay for their work. You couldn't find a Glatorian under every rock, of course, but now and then, you stumbled across someone with real potential — if you knew where to look.

A flash of light in the sky caught Metus's attention. At first, he thought it was a shooting star. But no, it was too bright for that. Some kind of meteor, maybe? The mysterious object was headed for the desert sands not far from Vulcanus.

For a moment, he dismissed the whole thing. It had nothing to do with him, after all. But then some instinct kicked in — the same instinct that had led him to amazing success so often in the past — and it told him to check this out. Maybe it wasn't just a hunk of rock from space . . . maybe it was something really valuable.

What are the odds? he said to himself, even as he drove in the direction of its likely impact. He shook his head, chuckling at himself. What was he thinking? With all of Bara Magna's troubles, did he really imagine the answer was going to fall down from the sky?

The glowing object screamed down from the heavens and crashed into the sands of Bara Magna, digging a trench in the charred ground. It came to a stop several yards from its point of impact, smoke rising from its still-white-hot surface.

Had anyone been present, they would have guessed that it was some kind of mask. It was golden in color and quite beautiful, despite having been through a long journey and an abrupt crash landing.

A native of Bara Magna would most likely have seen it as a potentially valuable item that could be traded for water or some other needed resource. Even if it was just ornamental, someone would want it to hang on the wall of their shelter. Maybe it could even be melted down and the metal used to make a tool or a weapon.

But the only living things around was a small army of desert beetles. Their only interest was to find out if the object was something they could eat. If it wasn't, they would most likely turn away and leave it where it lay. Over time, the sands would cover it, and its appearance would be quickly forgotten.

And if that happened, no one on all of Bara Magna would know that the salvation of their world had indeed fallen from the sky. . . .

THE LEGEND REBORN

*Take a special sneak peek
at the movie novelization!*

A swarm of scarabax beetles scurried across a sand dune, in search of their evening meal. On most evenings, this hunt was uneventful. The beetles would feed and then return to their underground tunnels. But this night was destined to be different.

One beetle lifted its eyes from the sand and saw something strange. It began clicking its pincers to alert its comrades. Other scarabax joined in, watching as a point of light streaked through the night sky and became a large fireball.

The scarabax scattered. The falling object smashed into the ground and skid across the sands, carving out a trench as it traveled. The intense heat fused the sand to glass. Finally, it came to a halt on the edge of a dune. Smoke drifted from its metallic surface.

Slowly, the scarabax emerged from hiding. They could feel the heat coming from the object. The swarm moved closer clicking their pincers rapidly, until they were surrounding this strange item. They didn't realize that it looked like a metal mask. Still, there was something about it which compelled them to draw near. . . .

Without warning, the mask rose into the air. The beetles jumped back in surprise as the sand beneath it rose like a miniature cyclone. Now the mask hovered more than seven feet in the air, surrounded by a contained sand-storm. After a few moments, the sands began to take on a recognizable shape. Two arms, two legs, and a torso formed from the whirling grains, then turned solid.

The storm ended. There now stood a being wearing a mask. His armor was white and gold, and his body lean and strong. He brought his hands to his mask, gently, as if not certain it was real. Then he looked down at his new body.

Toa gone mad. Then he reminded himself: *There are no Toa here! This is not your home.*

The creature attacked Mata Nui again. The shield moved to block its blows, making it angrier. Mata Nui rolled aside to avoid a strike. The beast's claws slashed deep marks in the stone where his head had been a moment before.

Okay, not good, thought Mata Nui. *If I stay on defense, I'll wind up in pieces.*

Mata Nui scrambled to his feet as the beast attacked again. The creature whipped its tail around, preparing to strike with its stinger. Mata Nui took a step back — and stumbled over a boulder, landing on his back in the sand. The creature hit the boulder with its stinger. The force of the impact was so strong that it shattered the rock and broke off the attacker's stinger tail. Screeching in pain, the beast ran off into the night.

Mata Nui lay on the sand and rested on his shield, trying to catch his breath. Carrying out his mission on this world was going to be even harder than he thought.

There was a bright flash of light. "What — ?" said Mata Nui, in surprise. When the light faded, his shield was gone, returned to the form of the little scarabax beetle.

Mata Nui smiled at the insect. "Before this day, I never needed help from anyone or anything. Thank you."

He gently lowered his arm toward the ground, to allow the insect to run free. "Well, little one, I spared your life and you saved mine," he said. "Shall we call it even and go our separate ways?"

The scarabax responded with the rapid clicking of its pincers. Mata Nui chuckled, saying, "Okay, easy, it was just a — "

Mata Nui heard a sound. He turned and saw a small, white-armored figure approaching in a land vehicle. The vehicle looked like it had been patched and repaired a dozen times using pieces from wrecks. Was this another attack? Mata Nui grabbed the broken tail of the beast and stood up. The scarabax scampered up to his shoulder and hid on the back of his neck.

The driver looked at Mata Nui, then at the impact crater left by the mask, and back at Mata Nui again. He raised a crystalline sword and said, "State your business."

Mata Nui did not relax his guard. "Just a traveler looking for the nearest city," he replied.

To Mata Nui's surprise, the driver lowered his weapon and broke into a grin. "Well, then you may as well start digging," he said. "Here on Bara Magna, you're bound to find the ruins of one or another."

When Mata Nui didn't react, the driver added, "That's a joke . . . . Right. Well, to answer your question, the nearest village is Vulcanus. I've got some business there if you want a ride. That is, unless you'd rather wind up captured by a pack of Bone Hunters, or worse, Skrall."

Mata Nui didn't know this being, but he seemed friendly enough. The alternative was walking through this vast desert, with no idea which direction to go. The driver smiled as he got into the vehicle.

"What are Bone Hunters and Skrall?" asked Mata Nui.

"No one you ever want to meet."

Suddenly the driver struck at Mata Nui, who blocked the blow with the stinger tail.

"Relax!" said the driver. "You've got a filthy scarabax on your back. I was just trying to knock the disgusting thing off."

"Thanks, but I like him right where he is," answered Mata Nui, with a trace of warning in his tone.

The driver shrugged. "To each his own. I'm Metus, by the way. Now hold on!"

Metus gunned the vehicle into motion and it shot across the desert sands. They traveled for a long time through the wastelands. There was little to see — just long stretches of empty sand occasionally broken up by bizarre structures that jutted up from the ground at weird angles.

"What happened here?" Mata Nui asked finally.

"Who knows?" answered Metus. "It's been like this as long as anyone can remember. But if I had to make a guess, I'd say it was probably — "

"Evil," said Mata Nui, softly.

Metus glanced at his passenger, then shrugged. "I was going to say 'earthquake,' maybe 'volcanic eruption,' but 'evil' works. Not from around here, are you?"

"No."

"I figured," said Metus. He pointed at the stinger tail Mata Nui carried. "It's clear you can fight if you can defeat a Vorox, and there aren't many Agori or even Glatorian who can do that."

"Agori?"

"Me. I'm an Agori," Metus said, smiling. "Although most aren't as good looking as I am. That's another joke. Truth is, we're just peaceful villagers trying to survive. Not like the Bone

Hunters. They're cutthroats who steal what little we've got left."

The outline of a village appeared up ahead. Mata Nui could hear the faint sound of a crowd cheering.

"Ah, good . . . sounds like we're just in time," said Metus.

"For what?"

Metus's answer was a broad smile. He drove their vehicle into the outskirts of the village, which to Mata Nui's surprise, seemed to be empty. From where, then, was all the cheering coming?

The answer came a moment later. The settlement was crude, built near an obviously active volcano. Light came from torches planted in the ground and red-hot magma oozed from cracks in the surface. In the center of the village was a poorly constructed arena. The citizens were clustered together, watching as two warriors — one in red armor, one in white — fought ferociously.

Metus halted the vehicle and got out. Mata

Nui followed. "Back in the day, villages settled disputes the old-fashioned way — by trying to destroy one another," explained Metus. "Very messy. Lots of clean-up. So we came up with a solution. Representatives from each village fight one-on-one . . . ."

Mata Nui could hardly believe what he was seeing. In his universe, Toa fought for justice, to save lives and protect the innocent. But this was something different. "You Agori use your best warriors for . . . sport?" he asked, unable to keep the distaste out of his voice.

"Not sport — problem solving. Much more honorable than slaughtering each other. And considerably more profitable." Seeing Mata Nui's cold expression, Metus added hastily, "Errr . . . not that I care about that sort of thing."

"C'mon, Ackar! Take him down!" yelled someone in the crowd.

"Get him, Strakk!" responded another.

Metus led Mata Nui to a box, in which three Agori sat. He pointed to the fighters. "The red warrior, Ackar, used to be the greatest warrior in all of Bara Magna. The white one is Strakk, from the ice village of Iconox."

An Agori, also in red armor, rose to greet Metus. "Ah, Metus. Glad you're here. Look at Ackar. I'm telling you, his days are numbered. I practically had to beg him to fight."

"Mata Nui, meet Raanu. He's the leader of this village. Mata Nui's new in town."

Raanu nodded at Mata Nui, then returned his attention to the fight. After a few minutes, he turned to Mata Nui and said, "What do you think?"

Mata Nui gestured toward Ackar. "He fights without fear. That is a rare quality."

"True enough. But he's lost his taste for battle," said Raanu. "And once a Glatorian loses heart, it's not long before he meets defeat after defeat and must be banished. No doubt that is why Metus brought you here tonight."

"I don't understand — "

"Ha, let's not get ahead of ourselves, Raanu," Metus said, cutting off Mata Nui. "There's plenty of time to find a new First Glatorian to take Ackar's place. By the way, did I mention that I recruit Glatorian?"

In the arena, Ackar was pressing his attack. He dodged a wild swing of Strakk's ice axe and responded with a blow from his own fire sword. The impact rocked Strakk and sent his shield flying out of his hand.

"This red warrior fights with the courage of a true Toa . . ." said Mata Nui.

Strakk swung his axe again, but once more Ackar dodged. Seeing an opening, the red-armored warrior slammed his shield into his opponent's midsection sending Strakk flying into the arena wall. His weapon dropped from his hand as he crumpled to his knees.

The crowd exploded. "He's done it! Ackar! Ackar!"

Ackar stood over his now unarmed opponent. "Concede and this goes no further."

Strakk looked at Ackar with undisguised hatred. Then he slowly lowered his eyes, muttering, "All right. You win."

Satisfied, Ackar turned away and went to

retrieve Strakk's fallen shield. "You leave with your honor intact, and I with your shield, in victory."

Behind him, Strakk grabbed his ice axe and hurled it at Ackar's back. A shout of warning from the crowd came too late. Ackar spun and managed to catch the brunt of the blow on his shield, but the impact knocked him backwards. He hit the ground, stunned.

Strakk, grinning, stalked toward Ackar and picked up his axe.

"You call this honor?" Mata Nui said to Raanu, angrily. "He was clearly defeated!"

"We're just Agori. We're not going to take on a Glatorian," Raanu replied. "The leader of his village will decide what needs to be done."

That's not good enough, thought Mata Nui. He leapt over the railing into the arena, a bright flash heralding the transformation of the scarabax into a shield once more. The sight startled the crowd. No one had ever seen a shield appear from thin air before.

"Interesting," Metus said to himself. "No wonder he's so fond of that bug. . . ."

Strakk hadn't noticed the new arrival. He was standing over the fallen Ackar, axe in hand, ready to deliver the final blow. "You're finished, old — "

Mata Nui dove, tackling Strakk. Both hit the ground, but the experienced Strakk made it to his feet first, axe at the ready.

"I'll cut you down for that, outsider!" the Glatorian growled.

Strakk struck. Mata Nui brought his shield up, but the power behind the blow knocked him right off his feet. Strakk pressed his attack, as Mata Nui desperately tried to block his strikes. It seemed obvious to everyone that Mata Nui had no chance.

Metus shook his head. "Too bad. I'd hoped he'd bring a decent price. . . ."

Mata Nui was on the ground now. Strakk stood ready to finish him off. Ackar had revived enough to see what was happening. "Strakk, no!" Ackar shouted. "Your fight is with me!"

"You're next, Ackar," Strakk answered. "He asked for it, and now he's going to get it."

Mata Nui brought out the stinger tail, hoping to somehow parry the coming blow. The crude weapon touched his mask, and again, there was a bright flash of light. In the next moment, Mata Nui no longer wielded a broken stinger, but a bright, gleaming sword.

The crowd gasped and Metus's eyes widened in shock. Strakk staggered back. "How in — ?"

Mata Nui seized the moment. He lashed out with a sweeping kick that brought Strakk down and caused him to lose his grip on the ice axe. Mata Nui leapt to his feet, holding the blade of his new weapon at Strakk's throat.

"Concede," said Mata Nui coldly.

"Fine . . ." Strakk growled.

"For all to hear!" snapped Mata Nui.

Strakk glared at Mata Nui for a moment before shouting, "I concede!"

The crowd went wild, their cheers shaking the arena. Ackar walked unsteadily to Mata Nui's side. Spotting Strakk's hand inching toward his axe, Ackar stepped on the weapon, saying, "Don't." The ice Glatorian rose and limped out of the arena.

"What will happen to him?" asked Mata Nui.

"For attacking after he conceded? Banishment. Iconox can't afford to send Glatorian without honor into the arena. Strakk will be reduced to living in the wastelands before the week is out." Ackar offered Mata Nui the ice warrior's shield. "Your victory. Your prize."

Mata Nui shook his head. "You won honorably. The prize of victory is yours."

"In that case . . ." Ackar tossed the shield aside as if it were garbage. "I've got plenty of shields."

Ackar turned to look at the crowd. Most of the Agori were already filing out of the arena, not even looking in his direction. "How quickly they forget," he said softly. "I am already an outcast."

"It's never too late to win them back," answered Mata Nui.

Ackar shrugged. "Perhaps. . . . I am in your debt, stranger."

Mata Nui said nothing. But he wondered if he had just found the most valuable treasure that might exist on this world: an ally.